✳ WALK THE WORLD'S RIM

OTHER BOOKS BY BETTY BAKER

Killer-of-Death
Little Runner of the Longhouse
The Pig War
Rat Is Dead and Ant Is Sad
The Shaman's Last Raid
The Treasure of the Padres

WALK

BETTY BAKER

THE WORLD'S RIM

Sonlight
Curriculum Ltd.

For a catalog of Sonlight Curriculum materials for the home school, write, fax, or e-mail:

Sonlight Curriculum, Ltd.
8121 South Grant Way
Littleton, CO 80122-2701
USA

In memory of Esteban
and all others who have walked
the world's rim

✷ CONTENTS

✳ WALK THE WORLD'S RIM

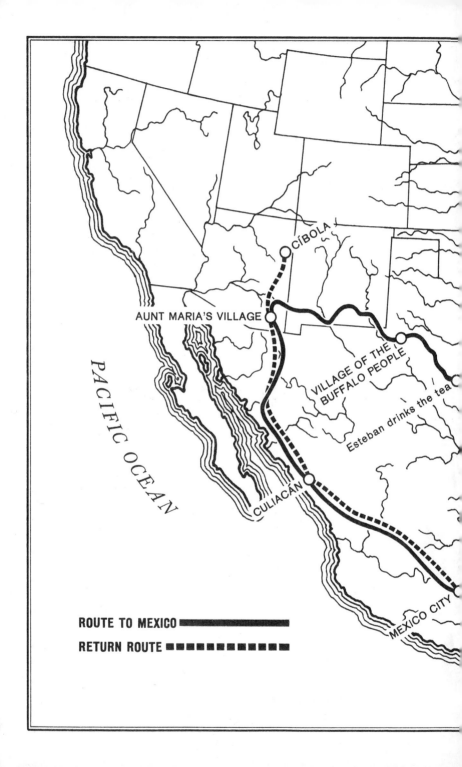

PACIFIC OCEAN

CÍBOLA

AUNT MARIA'S VILLAGE

VILLAGE OF THE
BUFFALO PEOPLE

Esteban drinks the tea

CULIACÁN

MEXICO CITY

ROUTE TO MEXICO ▬▬▬▬▬▬▬

RETURN ROUTE ▪▪▪▪▪▪▪▪▪▪▪

CHAKOH'S VILLAGE

GALVESTON

GULF OF MEXICO

TAMPA

ATLANTIC OCEAN

THE ETHEREDGES

✳ THE YEARS BEFORE

In the summer of 1527 five Spanish ships sailed from Cuba to explore Florida. The five Franciscan friars aboard hoped to convert the Indians to the word of God. The rest of the six hundred men dreamed of wealth. All but four of them found death.

The tragedy was the result of poor leadership. Against the advice of his best captains, Governor Pámfilo de Narváez led his soldiers inland, directing the ships to meet the army farther north. The soldiers never saw the ships again.

Beset by poisonous snakes, insects, treacherous swamps, and hostile Indians the Spaniards struggled north and west to what is now Pensacola. There, between Indian attacks, the men slaughtered their precious horses and used the hides to build crude boats. The barges pushed off for Mexico only to be separated by a storm at the mouth of the Mississippi River. A hurricane drove the three surviving barges ashore near what is now Galveston, Texas. In a futile attempt to launch the one salvaged barge, the men lost all their clothing, tools, weapons, and meager supplies.

Within a year sickness, starvation, and Indians diminished the survivors to four: Álvar Núñez Cabeza de Vaca, Alonso del Castillo Maldonado, Andrés Dorantes, and his Negro slave Esteban. Only four from more than six hundred men.

These four might not have lived either if they had not assumed the roles of medicine men. By blessings and prayers Castillo and de Vaca cured a great many Indians. Either the cures were miraculous, as the three Spaniards believed, or most of the illnesses were imaginary, brought on by fear of witches and spirits so that the patients easily imagined themselves "cured" by the Gods-From-the-Rising-Sun. Whatever the explanation, the more people they cured, the more closely the Spaniards were guarded. The Indians could not afford to let such valuable medicine men escape to another tribe.

For seven years the four men lived among the Gulf coast

Indians—primitive people on a near-starvation diet. Then late one summer they escaped and fled north into the unknown, unexplored interior of Texas. Without warm robes they could not survive the cold weather they knew was coming, so the Spaniards took refuge with the poor but friendly Avavare Indians.

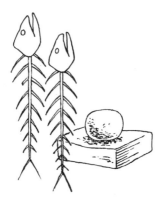

ONE ✵ IT GOES HUNGRY

The wind swept southward gathering cold and force over the arctic wastes. It roared through the canyons of the Rocky Mountains, started the buffalo herds drifting into its icy blast, and lashed the teepees of the Cheyenne. Then, its fury exhausted over the plains, the wind spent its last breath over the warm gulf where strange vessels sailed east and west. Familiar Indians or new-come Spaniards; teepee or caravel; it made no difference to the north wind. But to the Indian boy scuttling from a reed mat hut in the Texas hills each bone-chilling gust and rough splinter of sleet seemed sent by demons to plague him alone.

Chakoh pulled the skimpy deerskin tighter over his hunched shoulders. He lifted his head briefly to find the pair of huts set apart from the rest of the village. The bitter wind cut his squinted eyes, but the tears sprang as much from the painful hunger in his belly as from the icy air. Chakoh could not remember any comfortable length of time in all his fourteen years when he had not been cold and hungry. Except in the summer when he was hungry and hot.

The four Men-From-the-Sun spoke of a new god. They healed the sick with prayers to him. Perhaps he could stop the wind from blowing and bring food to the Avavares. Chakoh would gladly dance to any god or demon who could do such things. Then, fearful that the Spirit-of-Misfortune had read his thoughts, Chakoh spat twice over his left shoulder to honor and appease the malicious god.

He swept aside the stiff hide over the doorway of the hut and crawled through the low opening. Two men crouched over the fire pit. One was weathered as brown as Chakoh, but the hair growing long and thick on his face was the color of grass when there'd been no rain for many hot suns. Chakoh had seen the skin protected by that beard. It was as white as the other man's skin was black.

The white man's blue eyes turned questioningly toward Chakoh.

"The wind has blown visitors to my father's hut." Chakoh's father was headman of the village. All visitors stopped there.

"They are ill?" It was more a statement than a question.

"Yes, Cabeza de Vaca. All the people have heard of your power to heal."

"I will go." The man closed his eyes and moved his lips silently. He touched fingertips to his forehead, chest, and each shoulder. Then he rose stiffly.

"Go with God," murmured the black man.

Chakoh waited until the door covering fell into place behind the Spaniard. Then he turned to the Negro and spoke in faulty Spanish.

"How goes it, Esteban?"

The big man grinned. "It goes hungry, to be sure. Sit and I will give you another Spanish lesson. The words will drown the rumblings of my belly."

Chakoh squatted beside the meager fire and laid a package on the dirt floor.

"Ay, yi! Food!" But Esteban's expectant grin faded as Chakoh unwrapped the dirty matting. "Fish bones."

"Hush!" Chakoh glanced fearfully at the hut door. "We're lucky to have them. I buried them long ago to keep them from being stolen."

"To be sure. We've already found it safer to eat meat raw. Try to cook it and someone steals it from the spit before your nose has filled with the smell."

Meat . . . Chakoh sighed at the thought of that rare food. Of any food. Half of his fish bones he'd given to his parents. It was all any of them would have that day. Perhaps for many days.

Esteban lifted one of the three fish skeletons gingerly between his huge fingers.

"And how do we eat this magnificent banquet?"

"We grind them between stones and lick the dust from our hands. It isn't much but it may keep us from starving."

"To be sure." Esteban sighed heavily.

As they ground and licked, Chakoh wondered how to ask about this god to which Cabeza de Vaca and the two Señors in the other hut spoke. These Men-From-the-Sun were so thin and so nearly naked that it hardly seemed possible their god could be any more powerful than the ones Chakoh's people already feared. But perhaps this god was only a healing god and there were others for hunting.

Chakoh glanced sideways at Esteban. Esteban was larger than the white men. Indeed, he was larger than any man Chakoh had ever seen, but his skin hung loosely on his massive frame. Like the three Señors, Esteban never complained, but he was the only one who finished his meals with a sigh as if regretting there wasn't more. Also, he was the only one who offered friendship. He spent most of his time hunting or talking with Chakoh or teaching him the

Spanish tongue. But one thing Esteban disliked speaking of. This god of the three Señors. Chakoh would have to save his questions until Cabeza de Vaca returned from treating the sick man in his father's hut. Meanwhile the boy searched for a topic to lure Esteban into telling one of his fantastic stories.

"You Men-From-the-Sun do not seem to mind hunger," he ventured at last.

"After seven years with the Indians southward you get used to not eating. Half those people die every year from starvation."

"It is the same here. The cactus fruit ripens, the fish swarm upriver, or someone kills a deer. For a short time there is enough, but then comes hunger, and what morsels you find are snatched from between your teeth." Chakoh banged the last fish bone violently with the small stone. "I have seen some eat the ground itself."

Esteban nodded. "And they died of it."

"You have traveled far. Is it the same everywhere?"

"Everywhere we've traveled from Florida to here."

"And this place to which you travel now, what about it?"

"Ah, when we get to Mexico it will be different. We'll receive the welcome of conquering generals. Ah, the fiestas with banquets twice a day."

Chakoh leaned forward eagerly. "Banquets of what?"

"All the fruits of the Viceroy's gardens, honey cakes that

melt on your tongue, fine stews seasoned with chili peppers, Indian tortillas large as cartwheels . . ."

"And meat?" interrupted Chakoh. "Will there be meat?"

"To be sure, little one. There will be duck roasted on a spit, plump hens, suckling pigs oozing with fat, and whole legs of mutton."

Though Chakoh had been learning the Spanish tongue through the long winter, many words, such as *pig* and *mutton,* held no meaning for him. From Esteban's tone he knew they were delights beyond anything he'd ever known. What a marvelous land this Mexico must be. No wonder the Señors were so eager to return. Why had they ever left? Chakoh would never leave such a place.

"And do you know what I'll do at the banquet?" demanded Esteban.

"What?"

"I'll take a tiny bit of this." His thick fingers plucked an imaginary morsel from the air. "One bite of that. Just a leg of the chicken, thank you. And but a thin slice of mutton." He waved his arm grandly. "Throw the rest to the dogs."

Chakoh gasped. "Is this how you fatten the dogs to eat them?"

"No, little one. We don't eat dogs in our country, though we've eaten worse in yours, to be sure. No, I want the wonderful feeling of having so much food that I can throw it away."

The wind sifted through the reed matting and lifted

their rags as they sat thinking of the food Esteban had just imagined thrown to the dogs. Chakoh could not imagine so much meat. He could not imagine what it would be like to have enough just to fill his own stomach every single day.

At last Esteban's voice broke the silence. "And after I've stuffed myself so I can barely waddle, do you know what I'll do?"

"What?"

"I shall go to the bullfight. Ay, yi! What a sight that is."

"What is a bull?"

Esteban scratched his tightly curled hair. "Well, I suppose you could say it's a large deer, larger than four of your deer, with long curved horns. Ay, the bull is fierce in anger. He paws the ground and gores right and left with the horns. Like so." Esteban imitated the actions of a maddened bull.

"Oh, you mean a buffalo."

Now Esteban looked puzzled. "What is a buffalo?"

"An animal such as you describe."

"But we've seen nothing larger than a small deer."

"They seldom come this far south, but many seasons ago during a dry time three of them strayed down along the river. Far to the north there are more buffalo than there are stars in the sky. Or so I have heard."

"Ay, yi!" Esteban's eyes widened so that the whites shone brightly in the firelight. "All those cows. Why do you live here? Why don't you move north and hunt the cows? You'd have plenty of food."

"The buffalo are big and fierce, just as you said. We have trouble enough killing a deer. Besides, the buffalo belong to the people in the north."

"To be sure. But it is a shame that all that meat walks about up north while we sit here with our stomachs hugging our backbones."

Chakoh glanced shyly up at the man. "When we are cold and hungry like this, the old ones tell us stories so we'll forget."

"You don't want to hear it again, little one."

"Yes, tell me, Esteban. Tell me again how you come to be here."

"But you don't understand what I speak about."

"To be sure, but I like to hear."

The big head tilted back to let loose a rumbling laugh. Chakoh knew he had won. He clenched his knees to his chest and waited for the unbelievable tale.

It was true he did not understand about ships, the islands from which they'd sailed, or where this Florida was in which they'd landed. Even six hundred men were beyond his imagining, but the tragedy that only these four in his village were left was something he understood very well. Just as he understood the hardship of living for seven years as captives of the coast tribes to the south. Those tribes came often to the cactus harvest. They were hungrier than Chakoh's people and cruel beyond belief. Even the tales of the Buffalo People were not as horrible as the things Chakoh had seen among the coast tribes.

Usually the story of the homemade hide barges, the storms, and hostile Indians held Chakoh spellbound, but this day his thoughts kept returning to what Esteban had said about the buffalo. When he returned to his father's hut the words stung his mind as sharply as the sleet dug at his bare legs and unprotected face.

Why did his people live in this harsh thorny country when others to the north had plenty of meat? It was true that his people hadn't the weapons to hunt the buffalo, but all the tribes gathered in peace to share the cactus fruit harvest. Couldn't the Avavares have a share of the meat killed by the buffalo hunters? Or learn from them how to hunt the great beasts and what gods required sacrifice?

When he suggested this to his father, the headman was shocked.

"This is our land, my son," he said sternly. "The buffalo belong to the tribes of the north."

"But why can't we move?" insisted Chakoh.

"This is the land the gods gave us when the earth was new. So long as we remain on it, we are free to follow our own ways. Why then should we move?"

"To get food."

"What value is food if we must obey the laws of strangers? We are our own masters. And we shall have food when the cactus fruit ripens."

That was three round moons away. Until then there was nothing but what they could dig from the ground with their bare fingers and not even that if the sleet and cold wind did not stop.

Chakoh said nothing, but as Cabeza de Vaca prayed over the man lying on a mat in the corner, he turned Esteban's words over in his thoughts. It was true the buffalo belonged to other tribes and perhaps they would not be friendly to the Avavares, especially to one fourteen-year-old Avavare if he should try to go by himself. But what about Mexico, the land of the three Señors?

He must question Cabeza de Vaca. But before the Spaniard finished speaking with his god, Chakoh had fallen asleep.

The storm raged the next day and the day after. In all that time there was no food in the village.

"It is your doing," Chakoh's father told him. "Someday you will be headman in my place. Thus your thoughts of leaving our land have doubly angered the Spirit-of-Misfortune."

He opened his medicine pouch and cast the bones, singing softly over them.

Fearfully Chakoh spat twice over his left shoulder and resolved to put all thoughts of strange gods and lands from his mind. He succeeded during the days, but his nights were haunted by dreams of Esteban, looking much like a buffalo with his dark skin and tightly curled hair, throwing baskets of food to a pack of round-bellied dogs.

No longer did he enjoy Esteban's company. The things he wished most to hear he could no longer speak of. Each time one of the Señors came to share the fire, Chakoh was forced to leave. It was the only way to keep the burning questions from passing his lips. If he spoke or questioned, he might bring disaster to his people from the evil Spirit-of-Misfortune. But knowing all he did now, how long could he keep silent?

The moon grew fat and was again eaten by demons. The cactus flowered and the fruit formed. The Señors spoke of leaving soon and that night Chakoh was not troubled by dreams.

He did not sleep at all.

At the end of the long cold night he had reached a decision. When the dawn broke, he spat twice over his left shoulder and crept from the hut.

TWO ✳ QUESTIONS

Chakoh took Esteban to hunt cold-stiffened lizards. They dug at rocks and roots until their fingers bled. Esteban moved boulders that Chakoh would not have tried even if he were a man. When they turned home before dusk each had three large lizards hidden beneath his loincloth.

"Half for your family and half for mine," said Esteban.

"You mean to share them with me?"

"To be sure."

Chakoh had hoped some would be given to his parents

but had not dared to ask. It was because of Esteban that they had caught anything at all.

He trotted to keep pace with Esteban's long stride. "You will be leaving soon."

Esteban glanced down at him but said nothing.

"We will not share many more fires," Chakoh tried again. He grinned at Esteban's rumbling laughter.

"Very well, little one. Bring your share to cook with ours, though I don't know why you hold our friendship so highly."

Chakoh did not consider the three Señors friends, especially the disagreeable Dorantes. Don Castillo was gentle and a great healer, but he was weak and this was no country for a weakling. Cabeza de Vaca commanded respect, but that was not friendship. Only Esteban had given that. It was Esteban that Chakoh would miss, but today it was Cabeza de Vaca with whom he must speak. And the best time to speak great thoughts was after one had eaten well. Or as well as one could eat at the end of a hard winter.

He stopped briefly at his father's hut, not even waiting to bask in his mother's pleasure at the game he brought. The sight of hungry villagers gave him a feeling of guilt until he remembered how much they owed the three Spaniards. A few lizards would not begin to pay for what they'd done this winter for the Avavares.

As he helped prepare the meal in Esteban's hut Chakoh took a deep breath and asked again about the country of many feasts toward which the Men-From-the-Sun were struggling.

Esteban laughed. "Are you back to that again, little one? It's been so long that I thought you'd forgotten it."

"I have not forgotten. There is much I wish to know."

"Then ask."

"And you will answer?"

"To be sure. But let's have no talk of food when we are preparing a feast."

Chakoh dropped the questions he'd been going to ask and selected one that had bothered him all winter but he hadn't dared ask before.

"Do you really come from the land where the sun rises?" That was not the direction in which the Señors planned to travel. Surely they would want to return to the land from which they'd come.

Esteban's toothy grin disappeared. He looked beyond the fire into the shadowed corners of the hut.

"To be sure," he said at last. "I come from a land as near the place where the sun rises as you can travel from here."

"And is that why you are black, from being burned by the sun?"

"No, little one, I come from a land where all men are black, some blacker than I."

"I cannot believe it!"

The grin returned. "And I cannot believe you or any of your people, but you are here, to be sure."

Chakoh pondered a moment. "The three Señors are white. How did they come to be in your land?"

"I was taken to their land, Spain. It is near mine."

"But then what is this Mexico they say is toward the setting sun and then south?"

"It is hard to explain, little one."

Chakoh hugged his legs to his chest and waited. Esteban grinned at him and shook his head.

"I see that I must explain. It makes no difference that you will not understand."

Spain, ocean, ships, and islands were now familiar through Esteban's stories. Though he did not understand, Chakoh no longer worried over them. The great warrior Cortez and his conquest of the Aztecs was understandable. Chakoh had seen battles, but the city of Mexico and the kind of fighting done there astounded him. To think that such a great thing had happened when he was toddling around the village as a tiny child and his people had known nothing of it. But Esteban was right. He did not understand at all.

"If, as you say, the Spaniards already had a perfectly good land, why did they want another?"

"By the beard of the Prophet, is there no end to your questions?"

Chakoh ducked his head. "But you said you would answer."

"And so I will." Esteban chuckled. "But it would be

easier to tuck you under my arm and carry you to Mexico to see for yourself."

If only Esteban would do just that!

Cabeza de Vaca crept into the hut with something bundled in the front flap of his loincloth.

"I took Dorantes to dig roots. Most I gave to that widow with three children, but I saved enough for some sort of stew."

"Put them aside for tomorrow," said Esteban. "Tonight we have meat."

The Spaniard peered at the lizards roasting over the coals. "Don't tell me. Let me think it's quail. I'll enjoy it more."

The other two Spaniards crowded into the small hut. Castillo carried the rosary he'd made of brown and gray seeds. He sat in the shadows fingering the seeds and whispering prayers. Dorantes pushed up to the fire and rubbed his hands together in the warmth. He sniffed the food.

"What's that?"

"Don't ask," warned Cabeza de Vaca.

"The boy bring it?"

"Esteban caught them," said Chakoh.

Dorantes rubbed his hands tighter. "Esteban, eh? Best investment I ever made."

Esteban divided the meat into small flat baskets. When he passed them around, he added some of his own share to Castillo's.

"Here, here," said Dorantes. "None of that, Esteban. You eat your whole share. You're getting weak as it is."

Chakoh grinned, remembering the boulders Esteban had moved that day. He tried to catch his friend's eyes, but Esteban scowled down at his food as though Dorantes' concern annoyed him.

The men bowed their heads to speak with their god. Chakoh lowered his too but watched out of the corner of his eye. When they touched fingers to forehead, chest, and shoulders, he imitated the gesture.

Cabeza de Vaca saw him and smiled. "How goes the Spanish, Chakoh?"

"It goes well."

"And Esteban has been teaching you other things as well, I see. I'm surprised. It's too bad we haven't a priest here to continue the training."

"Priest?" Chakoh looked to Esteban for an explanation.

Esteban glanced at the Spaniards. "A medicine man," he replied in Avavare.

"But aren't the Señors medicine men?" Chakoh asked in the same tongue.

"No."

Cabeza de Vaca asked for a translation.

"He's asking about priests."

The Spaniard smiled. "One day a priest will come here and build a church."

"What is a church?"

Esteban grinned but let Cabeza de Vaca answer.

"It is the house of God."

That explained many things. At last Chakoh understood why the Señors were so hungry and had no warm deerskins and why their god had not rescued them from the coast tribes. Their god lived in a hut in Mexico. It was there that his strength was greatest. Here it was weak, so that the Señors could only ask him to heal. It was the same as carrying an ember in a clay pot instead of the large fire from which the ember had come.

He glanced around. Would a god live in a hut like this? "This is the largest of our huts, yet it seems small for a god."

Dorantes laughed. "The church in Mexico is so large you could put three of your villages in it."

Chakoh's eyes widened. "Who wove such big mats? How are they held up?"

"The church isn't made of mats. It's built of stone."

Dorantes' tone was scornful but Chakoh didn't notice. He was lost in wonder and amazement.

In his mind he pictured a small land closed off from the earth by a small sky. Inside this sky-topped cave was a plain covered with villages. Did it have its own sun and moon? It must. How else would there be light? Truly this god must be stronger than any the Avavares knew. Strong enough to overcome the Spirit-of-Misfortune that plagued his people.

"I should like to see this church and learn more of your god."

"Then why not come with us?" said Cabeza de Vaca.

"The journey is too long and harsh. He's only a boy," said Esteban.

"He's approaching manhood. Besides, he knows Spanish well and has already learned something of Christianity. I think his education should continue."

"He's too young," repeated Esteban.

Chakoh stared from one to the other. What was the matter with Esteban? Didn't he want Chakoh along? Esteban's next words removed all doubts of his friend's affection.

"His father is the headman. Chakoh is his only son. He will not let Chakoh leave the village."

"But I think he will." How could he refuse when he heard of these wonders? "If he agrees, may I go?"

"He'll be a burden to us, another useless mouth to feed." Dorantes glared at the praying Castillo.

Esteban scowled angrily at the Spaniard's grumbling. "A boy like Chakoh is never a burden."

"What could he do?"

"He knows how to live in this country. He's also quick with languages. He would make an interpreter if something should happen to me."

"Nothing will happen to you," shouted Dorantes. "Not unless I want it to."

The air in the hut was alive and threatening like that before a thunderstorm. Chakoh had felt the same atmosphere when quarreling headmen visited his father. He backed toward the deerskin. Someone murmured, "Go with God," as he scurried through the doorway into the clean friendly night. The relief of having escaped some unknown danger flowed over him. It was always like this when Esteban and Dorantes were together. As always, he wondered why, but did not dwell long on the mystery. He had a larger problem, persuading his father to let him accompany the Señors to Mexico.

It was far easier than he'd thought. He told of the little world their god had created inside a cave with a small sun and moon to light and guide it. His father nodded.

"In the beginning our people came from out of the earth. Perhaps that is the place from which they came."

"Then it would be well for me to return there."

"I do not know."

Chakoh put forth his last argument. "Someday I will be headman of our village. If there is a god strong enough to overpower the Spirit-of-Misfortune, it would be well for me to know of him."

"That is true." His father looked long into the fire. Then he said, "I will study the signs."

Chakoh lay on his sleeping mat watching his father's back. From time to time the man's arms jerked upward tossing the contents of his medicine bag on a flat basket. Then he leaned over and peered at the design before tossing again. Chakoh knew better than to try to sneak a look at the objects on the basket or to ask the mystery of the ritual. Each man had to discover his own medicine and the way to invoke its power. He only hoped the Spirit-of-Misfortune would not interfere.

He turned his head toward his left shoulder, changed his mind and made the sign of the Señors instead. Now was as good a time as any to begin. Then he turned over on the sleeping mat and let the spirits, good and bad, struggle with the contents of his father's medicine pouch.

In the morning he needed only one look at his father's sad eyes to know which had won. He raced off to give Esteban the good news.

After that came anxious days of waiting filled only by the desperate search for an ever dwindling source of food. The Spaniards had already decided to travel north. Mexico was to the southwest, but they feared the cruel coastal tribes and considered it safer to travel northwest until far beyond their former captors' reach. Besides, Chakoh had repeated what he knew of the buffalo. Food might be more plentiful to the north, and if the Avavares were an example, the tribes were certainly friendlier. The only question was when to leave.

"The cactus fruit is turning color," Cabeza de Vaca announced. "We'll have food for our journey now. We will leave."

Chakoh began to explain that the color meant nothing. It would be another moon before the fruit was ripe enough to eat. But he thought better of it. Food would be no harder to find farther north than it would be this next month in the village. Also, if they delayed until food was plentiful, his father might decide there was no need for a new god and change his mind about letting Chakoh go. An empty stomach had had much to do with his father's decision.

Chakoh slung his quiver over his shoulder, picked up his bow and stone ax, and went to join the Men-From-the-Sun in the center of the village. Esteban waited for him. He drew Chakoh to one side.

"You should not go, little one."

"I must. My father wishes me to learn of this new god."

"But it is not a new god. Listen to me, little one. God, Allah, Earth Maker, Spirit-of-Good-Things, it is all the same. Only the name is different."

"The Spirit-of-Misfortune and the Spirit-of-Good-Things are not the same."

Esteban sighed. "Chakoh, these are your people. This is your land. Stay here with those who care for you. Stay with the life you know. No land is like the land of your birth. No people like your own."

"That is true," said Chakoh bitterly. "What other place could be like this?"

Together they turned and looked over the village of reed-mat shacks, dirt piled around the north walls in a useless attempt to keep out the cold winter winds. Every bone could be counted in the naked chests of the people moving about in the weak sunshine. Children dug for roots. Two men fought over the carcass of a wood rat.

"Ay, yi!" breathed Esteban. "One forgets, but this is even worse than what I remember of—" He interrupted himself to land a hearty slap on Chakoh's shoulder. The boy sprawled on the ground.

"A thousand pardons, Chakoh." Esteban picked him up as easily as he would a roll of straw mats and stood him upright. "Dorantes has said so often I am weak that I'm beginning to believe him. Are you hurt?"

Chakoh shook his head.

"Then come. We're off to Mexico—the feasts and the bullfights."

The villagers walked along with the travelers begging them to stay and heal their sick, but the Spaniards were determined to go on. When the escort turned back, Chakoh said farewell to his parents.

On his chest his father wore a scalloped shell with mysterious symbols scratched on its smooth inner surface. The headman lifted the thong and placed it around Chakoh's neck.

"It will protect you, my son."

Chakoh embraced him. Then his mother looked long into his eyes. When she embraced him, her face was wet with tears. Chakoh turned quickly away before he too should weep and change his mind. Determinedly he trotted after Esteban, not looking back at the only home he had ever known.

Back there was only famine. Ahead lay Mexico with all its mysteries and the promise of a full stomach.

THREE ✳ STRONG MEDICINE

The Spaniards soon discovered the cactus fruit was not fit
to eat despite its red color. The milky juice burned their
mouths so badly they could not eat, even when the next
village had a few dried berries or stringy roots to offer.
The farther north they traveled, the greener the fruit became and the scarcer grew the food. Desperately Chakoh
broke off the round thick cactus pads and roasted them. It
was enough to keep strength in their legs. All except for

Don Castillo. Often Esteban had to carry him over the rougher places.

The fame of the three white medicine men had spread from tribe to tribe. Men or boys from each village guided them to the next one, sending word of the three Señors before them. The Indians gladly shared whatever they had, but each village seemed poorer than the one before. One thing in which they were rich . . . the sick. Often the Spaniards walked all day only to remain awake most of the night praying over those who came to beg for their blessings.

Day after day Chakoh trudged in Esteban's dust, feet bleeding and hunger gnawing. Was it for this he'd left his own land? Where was the wonderful Mexico? He'd lost count of how many suns they'd traveled, but it was taking longer than he'd expected.

"The earth is so big," he complained to Esteban. "It goes on and on as far as you can see, and when you get there, it goes on beyond that. I am beginning to believe it has no end. The earth goes on forever and probably on beyond that, too, as far as one can see."

Esteban chuckled. "To be sure, little one. The world is round. It is as if we were ants walking on the rim of a basket. If we walk on and on around the rim, we will come back to where we started."

"Then surely we'll reach my home again soon."

"No, little one. It is not that easy. I know."

"How long does it take then?"

Esteban strode along, head down in thought. Chakoh reached out and tugged his hand.

"Esteban!"

The man jerked as if startled from sleep. "What is it?"

"How long does it take to walk the rim of the earth?"

"I do not know. Always the Spaniards have brought me west, but never have I seen the home of my parents. Never since I was like you, little one." He rubbed the top of Chakoh's head gently and sighed. "Perhaps there are some who must walk the rim forever."

He returned to his walking dream.

The boy trotted along lost in his own thoughts. This would be a longer journey than he'd thought. Like Esteban he might reach manhood before he returned. It was a matter that required a great deal of thought.

That night, before a meal of nuts and rabbits, the villagers told them of the next town. The people there spoke a different tongue. Yes, there were some in the village who could teach the strange words. They were slaves taken in battles long ago, but they still remembered.

Chakoh drew himself to his full height. "I will not share a cookfire with slaves."

His companions stared at him. Dorantes laughed harshly. Cabeza de Vaca silenced him with an angry glare.

"You need not eat with them," said de Vaca. "Just learn their native tongue."

The three Señors followed the chattering Indians. Chakoh turned to Esteban.

"Tell them we won't do it."

Esteban turned and strode away.

"Esteban, wait! You cannot sit with the slaves."

"And why not?" He did not slow his pace. Chakoh stumbled and had to run to catch up.

"They are men of no honor. They would rather be slaves than die like true warriors, and they did not care if the world knew of their fear. Their hearts are weak. They have no sense of shame, for they surrendered rather than fight."

Esteban halted. "Perhaps they did not have a chance to fight."

"Then they should have refused to do the work of slaves. They should have forced their masters to kill them by trying to escape."

"That is what you would do, little one?"

"Yes," Chakoh shouted. "A headman's son must protect his honor even more carefully than he protects the secret of his medicine."

"But perhaps a slave protects his honor by obeying his master's commands. Perhaps that takes great courage also."

Chakoh spat contemptuously. "No man of courage and honor becomes a slave."

Esteban stared down at him, a great sadness in his dark eyes. Chakoh ducked his head, then raised it defiantly.

What he had spoken was the truth. It must be, for it was what he'd been taught. His people had nothing of value but their freedom. It was to protect it that they lived in the harsh land the gods had given them. Yet had he not wished to leave that land, to join the Buffalo People? But not as a slave. He would still have had his freedom. It was one thing a warrior could not live without. There was no greater shame and dishonor than slavery.

"And what of me, little one?" Esteban's voice was almost a whisper. "Have I no honor or courage?"

"No man has more, not even Señor de Vaca. I would not be here if you were not going to Mexico too."

Esteban walked slowly a short distance and stood gazing at the darkening sky. Chakoh thought back over his words. No, it could be nothing he had said that caused the great shoulders to slump as if in sorrow. At last the shoulders straightened. Esteban turned and walked briskly back to Chakoh.

"Come, we must learn this new tongue." Chakoh began to protest but Esteban shouted him down. "Have you so little courage that you are afraid to speak to slaves across the fire? Have you so little honor that you would refuse the request of the Señors?"

"It is not a matter of courage and honor. I just don't wish to be near such men." Chakoh sighed. "But if you go, I will go also."

They sat late by the fire learning what words they could of the new language. Esteban had a gift of tongues. For

Chakoh it was harder. He was not easy in the presence of the two slaves. Also he had other things to think of.

As he listened and murmured the new words to himself Chakoh cut a wide strip from the front flap of his loincloth. He punched holes in the edges with a bone awl and carefully sewed the strip into a pouch. For thread he used thongs cut from the loincloth. More thongs were cut to make drawstrings. It was slow work, but he had finished by the time the slaves left them.

Chakoh rose and stretched.

"By the beard of the Prophet!" Esteban stared at Chakoh's loincloth. "What have you done?"

Chakoh glanced down. The strip of old deerskin ran between his legs and draped over a thong tied around his waist. The ends had hung, front and back, almost to his knees. Now the front panel came less than a hand's breadth below the thong. Another stretch and it might come loose altogether.

"I needed deerskin."

"Are you that hungry? Ay, yi! We'll all be naked before we reach Mexico. I can see you chasing Dorantes over the hills, screaming for his last strip of loincloth." He rolled his eyes upward in mock horror.

Chakoh grinned in spite of himself. "Be serious, Esteban."

"But I am. You had better even those flaps a little before you disgrace the Señors."

"No! What would I sit on?"

"You should have considered that before you hacked the loincloth."

"But I need a medicine bag. If I am gone from home as long as you, I shall need strong medicine. It is time I began to gather it."

The big head nodded solemnly. "To be sure, little one. Let us make a trade."

"Trade?" He glanced down. Surely his shortened loincloth would be twice as shocking to the Señors on the enormous Esteban.

"This is the trade. You rearrange your loincloth and bear the discomfort for a short time. When we come to a village with deerskin to trade, I shall get you a new one. Agreed?"

It was a good bargain. He would have a fine new loincloth plus all the deerskin left in his old one. He would be wealthy and all he need do in return was remember to clear the ground carefully before he sat.

"Agreed."

He hung the empty medicine pouch on the thong around his waist and lay down wondering when he'd find medicine strong enough to fill it. Perhaps Don Castillo would give him some of the praying seeds. No, the Spaniard needed those. He would have to find something else.

He curled up against Esteban's broad warm back and fell into a restless sleep. Now that he'd thought of gathering his medicine against the Spirit-of-Misfortune, he could no longer feel safe until he found some.

Two days later they arrived at the village of the People Who Were Different. Their guides explained to the new Indians that the three white men were great healers from the rising sun. The women welcomed them, said they had heard of the great healers, and explained that the men were fasting for a ritual. When it was over, three days from now, some of the men would gladly guide the Señors over the mountains.

"Ask how long they've been fasting," whispered Cabeza de Vaca.

Esteban translated.

"Two days," was the woman's answer.

"Then there's been no hunting in all that time." The Spaniard sighed. "We must make the best of it."

He blessed their guides and sent them home.

Huge covered pots boiled on the fires. Chakoh lifted a lid and the stench of the yellow tea gagged him. A woman shrieked at him to get away. The tea was part of the ritual, and he might destroy its magic. He hurried off to share a watery stew with the men.

The village was quiet.

"Too quiet," said Dorantes. "I don't like it."

They took turns watching through the night. Nothing happened until dawn, when painted men leaped from the silent huts and sat around the fire shouting, "Who wants to drink?"

One of the pots of evil-smelling tea went around. Each

man gulped until Chakoh's throat ached from watching. The fifth man to drink became violently ill.

"Some woman has looked in the pot and poisoned it," shouted the men.

The woman who'd chased Chakoh pointed at the four strangers. He could not understand her jabbering, but there was no mistaking her meaning. She was blaming him for "poisoning" the tea. The men around the fire turned to scowl at him. Their black and white painted faces sent chills up Chakoh's spine. He groped for his medicine bag but it was still empty.

"This is the end," said Dorantes. "I knew that boy would be trouble. He's killed us all."

"Not yet," said de Vaca. "Have faith. Something will save us."

Castillo fingered his rosary, lips moving.

"Ay, yi!" Esteban jumped up and ran to the circle. He leaped over the head of a seated Indian and pranced around the "poisoned" pot of tea in short hopping dance steps. All the time he chanted short jerky phrases of Spanish.

Chakoh glanced at the Señors. Cabeza de Vaca and Dorantes were having difficulty keeping straight faces. Castillo seemed not to hear Esteban.

"One melon, two melons, hurry get some more. The merchant went home and left me to guard the store." Esteban waved his big hands back and forth over the pot as he repeated the chant. Then he seized the enormous earthen jug and lifted it to his mouth. Seven times his throat worked before the jug lowered. Esteban stood rigid. His eyes bulged as if trying to escape from his head. Sweat beaded his forehead. Then he swallowed hard and yelled, "Ay, yi!"

"Ay, yi!" repeated the painted Indians. One grabbed the jug from Esteban's hand and shouted, "Who wants to drink?"

Esteban staggered over to Chakoh and sank heavily to the ground.

"Castillo must have prayed for me," he croaked. "Only a miracle could keep that witches' brew down."

The miracle was only temporary. In a few moments Esteban was heaving worse than any of the Indians. They kept him out of sight but only because everyone was occupied with the ritual around the fire. Each time an Indian became sick and a woman was threatened with a beating, the Spaniards held their breaths. If one of the women fled in their direction, she would surely discover Esteban retching behind the hut. The Indians would be certain the tea had been poisoned by Chakoh.

By night they had a greater worry. Esteban was too weak to stand. He waved away all food and water and just lay breathing in short gaspy puffs.

"Maybe it *was* poisoned," said Dorantes.

Screams rose from the center of the village.

"The men think it's poisoned," said Chakoh. "They are beating one of the women for looking at their tea."

"Soon all the women will have fled into the darkness. The next time a man becomes ill, they'll have no one to blame. They'll come looking for us."

Cabeza de Vaca pulled at his beard. "For once, Dorantes, I believe you are right. We must go on. If we stay here, they may turn on us."

"But we have no guides."

"There is a trail. We can follow it over the mountains."

"But Esteban," cried Chakoh. "We can't leave Esteban."

"It's him or us," growled Dorantes.

"It is all of us or none." De Vaca's tone left no room for argument. He bent over Esteban. "How goes it?"

"It goes easier. No!" He waved a limp hand. "No food. Just let me rest. I will be on my feet before dawn. That I promise."

"Do you think he will?" whispered Chakoh.

"If Esteban promised, he will do it."

They huddled together listening to the chants growing wilder as the night lengthened. Well before dawn Cabeza de Vaca roused them.

"It is time. Let us go."

Esteban pushed himself to hands and knees, rested a moment, then rose to his full height. He swayed unsteadily, reaching out his arms for balance. Chakoh slipped under the left arm. The weight on his shoulders was as great as that of a full-grown deer, but he stiffened his knees and supported the tottering Esteban as they moved silently from the village. Exercise seemed to help Esteban. By midday he was able to take turns leading the way into the mountain pass, eyes ever seeking the dim trail.

Chakoh trailed behind, eyes also on the ground but not on the trail. When they stopped that night, he showed Esteban his medicine pouch full of shiny pointed leaves.

"These are what the women back there were roasting to make the tea. If they use it in their ceremonies, it must be strong medicine."

"To be sure. I never drank any that was stronger."

Chakoh nodded in satisfaction. His pouch bulged, but when they reached a campfire he would parch the leaves and crush them. Then there would be room for other magic. If one medicine was powerful, three or four must be even stronger.

The next day their path turned downward.

"Now that we are over the mountains," said Cabeza de Vaca, "the rivers should no longer flow south to the gulf. They should run west toward the Great Sea. That will mean we're past the gulf and can safely turn south toward Mexico without fear of the coast tribes."

"Look." Chakoh pointed north at the gray blanket of rain moving swiftly toward them. Thunder rolled. Lightning reached down to dance among the rocks. They left the path and groped along the mountain for shelter. Chakoh could not tell how far they stumbled over boulders and crept along ledges before they found a small cave where they huddled and shivered through the night.

Dorantes was the first to poke his head outside at dawn.

"Ha, so we're safely away from the coast, are we? Let me tell you, de Vaca, we've a good many more mountains to cross before that."

They crawled onto the rocky shelf and peered down. A river, flooded by the storm, churned through the wide valley below.

"It flows south," murmured de Vaca. "Into the gulf."

"A thousand thanks for calling it to my attention," sneered Dorantes. "Just how much farther is Mexico?"

"Only God knows."

The talk of rivers and directions meant nothing to Chakoh. He stared open-mouthed at the northern end of the valley. A great city spread before them less than a day's journey away. Never had he seen such strange huts nor so many. Eight times he counted all his fingers and still there were more of the tall tapering dwellings.

Without waiting, he led the way down the mountain and along the river. Esteban loped beside him. The three Spaniards lagged in the rear. Chakoh felt neither hunger nor fatigue. Surely this was the great city of Mexico at last.

But the people who came to greet them were Indians. Strangely dressed, but Indians just the same.

Chakoh stared at the robes draped over the shoulders of

the men. He edged closer to Esteban.

"The Buffalo People," he whispered fearfully.

All the stories he'd heard came flooding back. The Buffalo People tortured their own flesh in strange rituals to the sun. Their strong medicine protected the buffalo from strangers with whom they were not overly friendly. Their moods changed with the wind. For no reason at all they would attack people to whom they had been friendly.

Trembling beside Esteban, Chakoh fingered the deer-skin pouch. What use were the medicine leaves against these strong, grim-faced people?

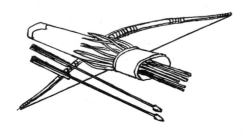

FOUR ❋ THE BUFFALO PEOPLE

Esteban and Chakoh tried all the dialects they knew and were finally reduced to using signs. They weren't sure the Indians understood, until they explained that the Spaniards following were great medicine men. Then the Buffalo People murmured and glanced at an old man standing cross-armed before a large painted teepee. Chakoh shivered. The Buffalo People had strong medicine of their own. Their medicine man would not welcome new gods.

The three Señors soon appeared on the trail. Dorantes and Cabeza de Vaca supported Castillo between them. The Buffalo People's medicine man snorted contemptuously and turned away. The other Indians crowded about the strangers, touching and rubbing their skins. Some even scratched Esteban to see if the black was painted on. Cabeza de Vaca stood quietly as his straw-colored beard was pulled, fingered, and whispered about. They bore it all patiently, for the Buffalo People had plenty of food. Dried meat, dried berries mixed with fat, and stew made of both.

Chakoh ate his fill, but, like the four men, his stomach was too used to a starvation diet to take more than one small meal a day. He tucked a strip of dried buffalo meat in his waistband for the time when his stomach stretched.

"Do you think we will stay here a while?" he asked Esteban.

"Who knows? Don Castillo needs the rest and food, but the people . . . " He shrugged his dark shoulders.

Chakoh nodded solemnly. The Buffalo People had not welcomed them joyously, as the other tribes had done. They gave the strangers food and shelter that courtesy demanded but not in the spirit of friendship. They kept their distance and seemed to be only waiting for an excuse to declare the Spaniards enemies.

Through the thin walls of the teepee Esteban and Chakoh could hear Dorantes arguing with Cabeza de Vaca.

"They don't like us," he was saying. "Have you noticed the way they finger their bows? Just waiting to put an arrow in our backs."

"Be that as it may," came de Vaca's calm voice, "Castillo can't go on without food and rest."

"Esteban can carry him."

"Esteban is not a horse."

"He can carry Castillo to the next village."

"What makes you think the people there will be any friendlier? We've traveled beyond our fame as medicine men."

"Then it's time we left this part of the country as quickly as possible. The next tribes may be friendlier."

There was a long silence.

"Very well, we will continue in the morning." De Vaca's straggly beard appeared under the teepee flap. "Esteban, will you ask the Indians for guides?"

Chakoh followed his friend through the camp. Esteban signaled their need for a guide to lead them to the next village across the river. The Buffalo People followed the hand movements with blank stares. Chakoh felt sure they understood. They simply did not think enough of the Señors to spare hunters for a trip. They cared nothing for what happened to these strangers. Chakoh could not blame them. If the Spaniards had not helped the sick and starving, his people would have felt the same.

"Now we must stay," Chakoh said.

Esteban shook his head. "Dorantes will insist we leave without a guide."

"But we don't know the trails."

"No matter. Does a frightened rabbit care where he runs?"

Chakoh glanced at their teepee, now close enough to see the Spaniards' shadows through the oiled sides. He lowered his voice. "Castillo will not be with us long if we move tomorrow. I know. I have seen many like him."

"To be sure." Esteban looked as if he would say more but didn't.

Chakoh knew what he was thinking. If they stayed, there was a chance none of them would leave the village. When they approached the Buffalo People, the tension and mistrust were almost strong enough to touch. He fingered the dried meat in his waistband, but his stomach felt too uneasy for food.

Esteban's heavy hand ruffled the boy's hair. "Report to the Señors, little one."

"And you?"

His only answer was to squeeze Chakoh's shoulder, then disappear into the darkness at the edge of the camp.

The boy hesitated, tempted to follow, but Esteban had commanded him to report. With a sigh Chakoh entered the teepee and told of their failure to find a guide. After a heated argument it was decided that they'd ford the river in the morning, Esteban carrying Castillo on his back.

Cabeza de Vaca crossed himself. "And may God guide our footsteps."

The words were no sooner out when a babble of voices rose in the village. Chakoh was first out of the teepee. The crowd of Indians halted at sight of the Spaniards. Esteban hobbled forward and leaned heavily on Chakoh's shoulder. Blood trickled from two small marks on his right calf.

"What happened?" asked Chakoh.

"Get me into the teepee. Quickly!"

Before Chakoh could move the chattering crowd of Indians parted. The Buffalo medicine man stalked up to Esteban. A warrior stepped forward to explain in words and signs. The medicine man smiled. His eyes narrowed as he turned to Esteban and made the cutting sign of death.

"What did he say?" asked Dorantes. "What's wrong with Esteban?"

Chakoh shook his head. His throat was too numb to pass words. Through blurred eyes he helped Esteban into the lodge and lowered him gently to the buffalo robes. Dorantes tagged behind plucking at Chakoh's arm and getting in the way.

"What is it, boy? What's the matter with him?"

Anger released Chakoh's voice. "Esteban was bitten by a rattlesnake."

"How could he be so careless?" shrieked Dorantes. "I should have him whipped."

Chakoh gaped at the angry Spaniard. "Don't you understand? Esteban will die."

"He can't. I won't let him."

Cabeza de Vaca pushed past the babbling Spaniard and looked down at Esteban's leg.

"Two horses," continued Dorantes. "That's what he's worth, and you know horses in this country are beyond price. He can't die. He's all I have left. The Indians must know some herb to use. Boy, don't you know any medicine?"

He grabbed for Chakoh, but Cabeza de Vaca stepped between them.

"Get out, Dorantes. Do you hear me? As the surviving senior officer of this expedition, I order you to get out."

Dorantes backed slowly from the teepee. Castillo shuffled after him, saying, "I will pray for his soul."

The muttering of the waiting Indians could still be heard. There was no sorrow in their voices, just curiosity and an occasional ripple of laughter.

Cabeza de Vaca knelt by Esteban. "Some light here, Chakoh." He sighed. "If only we had a sharp Toledo blade."

"It is too late for a knife," said Esteban.

"True, my friend. Only one of Castillo's miracles can save you now. Why did you wander from the camp at night? You know the serpents roam after sunset."

Chakoh brought a flaming branch from the fire and knelt across from de Vaca. He gasped and leaned closer. His eyes raised to meet the Spaniard's.

"There should be swelling by now or ugly streaks. It *is* a miracle."

"Is it?" The Spaniard touched the two bloody marks. "Have you ever seen snakebite bleed so freely? Or leave such jagged marks?"

They turned to Esteban, who was propped on his elbows grinning at them.

"I said it was too late for a knife. I needed one when I cut. A stone knife makes too large a hole. That is why I needed to get into the teepee quickly. The Indians must continue to believe a snake has bitten me."

Cabeza de Vaca sat back on his heels. "I don't know whether to weep from relief or to let Dorantes whip you."

"Why?" asked Chakoh. "Why did you do it?"

"To make the Señors great medicine men again. To be sure, the Buffalo People will never bring anyone for them to heal, but now they can heal me. And what a great healing it will be. Something not even their own medicine man can do."

"And while we are healing you," said de Vaca, "Castillo can rest. It is a good plan, Esteban."

"If they believe Esteban was really bitten," said Chakoh.

"Just listen to Dorantes. The way he's carrying on out there, can there be any doubt?"

Esteban sighed. "I suppose we must tell him the truth."

It was decided that Chakoh would announce that the Señors would perform a great healing. In three days, at sundown, Esteban would appear alive and well, cured by the great medicine men from the Land of the Sun.

"Go now," said Cabeza de Vaca.

Chakoh hesitated. He did not feel easy with the plan but could discover no reason. Perhaps it was only the aftertaste of his fear of losing Esteban. He rose slowly.

"I will try to make them understand."

He was not as good with the sign language as Esteban, but the Buffalo People understood. During the next days they went out of their way to pass the Spaniards' teepee. Women cleaning and stretching hides glanced often at the teepee as they talked. Groups of warriors stood about waiting to see if the strangers could indeed cure the bite of a rattler.

The Spaniards were busy "healing" Esteban. In this idle time Chakoh parched the tea leaves, replaced the dried remains in his medicine pouch, and kept his eyes open for strong medicine to add. Each day the Buffalo People hung their medicine bags on pronged sticks before their teepees. Chakoh wandered about the village, itching to see what the long hide cylinders contained but not daring to touch or even ask.

Late on the second day he stood wondering at the meaning of the quillwork design on one of the medicine bags.

Was it part of the medicine, or did it keep the magic powers safely inside the bag? The women came to carry the medicine bag inside the lodge for the night. Chakoh turned away and stopped.

The Buffalo medicine man stood before him. Silence fell over the camp. Women stopped chattering. Men moved close. Even the big yellow dogs stood expectantly, ears alert and tongues lolling.

Chakoh waited.

The medicine man pointed to the setting sun and raised one finger. *One more day for the Señors to practice their healing.* Then came the death sign. *Esteban will die.* The medicine man spun on his heel and strode away.

While aware of the signs, Chakoh had also searched the eyes of the medicine man. He had read the fear and anger in them, had all but heard the man's thoughts. Chakoh's knees trembled, but he forced himself to walk slowly past the staring Indians to his own teepee. He lifted the flap and hesitated.

"I can hardly wait to see their faces when you walk out of here tomorrow night," Dorantes was saying. "I never thought we'd get out of here with our skins whole. You're a smart one, Esteban. When we get to Mexico, I'll see you're properly rewarded."

Chakoh stepped away from the entrance. He'd forgotten about Dorantes. Even when he'd thought Esteban was dying, the Spaniard had babbled about horses and threatened to whip him. He had even spoken of abandoning Esteban in the village of the tea drinkers in order to save his own life. What would he do when he discovered that Esteban's plan was, like a rock thrown high into the air, about to come down and crush them all? Would the Spaniards even understand their danger?

Chakoh doubted it. The uneasiness he'd felt when Esteban told of his plan had not been felt by the Spaniards. They did not understand about medicine men, or they'd never treat their own power so lightly.

The Buffalo People had strong medicine. Their medicine man would be stronger and more powerful than those of Chakoh's people. The greater the power, the greater the fear of losing it. In the eyes of the medicine man Chakoh had read that fear. If the Spaniards "healed" Esteban of the snake bite, the Buffalo medicine man would be forced to destroy the Spaniards. He might call the Spirit-of-Misfortune down upon them or use some poisonous herb known only to himself. Whatever the magic he used, the result would be the same. He would have proved his medicine was stronger than that of the Spaniards, for Esteban and the Señors would be dead. Chakoh was not sure of his own fate. He hoped it would be the same as Esteban's. Rather death than the disgrace of slavery.

"It does not matter," he muttered to himself. "I won't let it happen."

Esteban had saved him once by drinking the tea. Somehow he would save Esteban. But how?

He crushed the dried leaves in his medicine bag and sighed. What good was that? The Buffalo People had stronger medicine. Besides, he had not yet devised a ritual for the use of the dried leaves.

His hands searched his nearly naked body. The Buffalo People had better bows and arrows. The cut loincloth was useless even to himself. Then his right hand cupped over the shell on his chest. Slowly he nodded. Hadn't his father said it would protect him?

Quickly he crossed himself in the magic sign of the Señors. Then, to be sure, he spat twice over his left shoulder before slipping the thong over his head. With the shell in his hand he marched across the shadows of men and teepees straight to the painted lodge of the Buffalo medicine man.

FIVE ✵ THE CURE

The Spaniards had already finished their evening meal. Esteban lay under the robes groaning and suffering for the benefit of the Indian woman who cooked and served them. Chakoh thumped down beside the fire and reached eagerly for his bark container of stew. Already his stomach was accustomed to two meals a day, and he had hopes of persuading it to accept a third.

"Be sure to leave some for the sick one," Cabeza de Vaca warned in Spanish, glancing cautiously at the Indian woman's broad back, as if seeing his lips would help her understand.

Chakoh grinned. "Our sick one won't be eating tonight."

Before he could explain, a piercing shriek prickled their skins. The entrance flap swept aside. In leaped a man striped with white paint. From a furred and feathered headdress rose two curved horns.

"By all that's holy," yelled Dorantes. "It's the devil himself."

"It's the medicine man. I asked him to help cure Esteban."

Actually Chakoh had said that the Señors were failing in their cure and begged the medicine man's help. Only his magic, added to their own, could save Esteban. Chakoh's fingers ached from the amount of sign talking he'd done. He'd had to heap flattery on the medicine man to make up for having only a shell of uncertain power as payment.

Dorantes turned on the boy. "Now you've ruined everything."

With a shaking of rattles and shrill chanting the medicine man danced slowly around Esteban. Chakoh moved closer to the Spaniards to be heard over the noise.

"It had to be done, Señors. The medicine man was envious. If we hadn't asked for his help, he would have made things very difficult for us."

Dorantes snorted. "I don't believe it. The Indians would have been awed by our powers."

Even Cabeza de Vaca looked doubtful.

"He might have said your medicine came from an evil spirit and ordered you killed as men possessed by demons. It has happened in my own village."

Cabeza de Vaca nodded. "You are right, Chakoh. We should have considered his envy and what it might lead to. You did well."

"And I guess that one isn't so clever after all." Dorantes glared at Esteban, who was mouthing words at Chakoh.

How long? he was silently pleading with glances at the performing medicine man.

Until sundown tomorrow, Chakoh signed back.

"And nothing to eat?" Esteban yelped aloud in Spanish.

"Not a bite. You are dying, remember?"

Esteban rolled back moaning in true misery. Chakoh grinned and scraped up the last of the stew with his forefinger.

With a sigh Cabeza de Vaca pushed himself to his feet. "We had better do our part."

The Spaniards knelt beside Esteban. As the medicine man's thin voice rose and fell in high keening tones, the Señors sang lustily of love, heartbreak, battles, and even one song about a faithful horse. Chakoh enjoyed what he could understand until Esteban began to twist and moan.

His eyes rolled back in the sockets. His arms struck at invisible enemies. His shrieks rose higher than those of the medicine man.

Chakoh had seen many of his people like this when the Spirit-of-Misfortune had breathed upon them. He clutched at the empty place on his chest. In trying to help had he brought destruction to Esteban by giving away the magic shell? Or was Esteban to be punished because they were tricking the medicine man and making a game of his powers?

He crept into a shadowed corner of the teepee and loosened the drawstrings of his medicine bag. He had not thought or planned but he knew exactly what to do. Crumbling the dried leaves between his fingers he made the Circle of Life on the hard packed earth. In the center he drew the wings and claws of the eagle and beneath them a coiled snake. Eyes closed, he added his chants to those of the medicine man, letting the words form in his heart and fly through his lips to the high air where the eagle soared.

"Chakoh!"

He jumped. The crack around the entrance flap showed light with the false dawn. The teepee was silent. He rubbed his numbed legs and hobbled to where Esteban lay motionless under the robes. The Spaniards looked pale and haggard, but the medicine man waited patiently, ready to continue through the day if necessary.

"Is he . . ." Chakoh could not force the fatal words past his lips.

"He's just exhausted by his performance," said Cabeza de Vaca. "You must tell the medicine man to go."

"What shall I say?"

"Anything," snapped Dorantes. "Just get him and his caterwauling out of here, so we can sleep."

"Then you must talk. Say anything, just so it appears I am repeating your words in signs."

It took a while but Chakoh made the old man understand that the good and evil spirits had retired from battle. At sundown they would know which had won. Until then they could do nothing but wait.

With a last shake of the rattle over Esteban's body, the medicine man left. Castillo stretched out where he was, but the other two rose stiffly to their feet. Esteban opened his eyes.

"You are cured," shouted Chakoh.

"To be sure, but a man can't sleep on an empty stomach. Have you left anything for me, little one?"

Chakoh rummaged in his robe for the little store of dried meat he'd put aside. Cabeza de Vaca watched Esteban gnaw on the tough meat.

"This makes me wonder," he said. "This is exactly the way the Indians that we cured acted."

"My people always behave like this after the Spirit-of-

Misfortune breathes on them," said Chakoh. "I have seen it often. So have you."

"Yes, we have. Does it always come and go so suddenly?"

"The Spirit-of-Misfortune always strikes suddenly, but almost always the medicine man cures my people."

"I see now that we might have saved our prayers and vows. We are not the great healers that we thought."

"But you are," said Chakoh. "Our medicine men never cured them as quickly as you."

"And I imagine they never had quite as many patients either. Never mind, Chakoh. I am thinking aloud."

Dorantes growled from the edge of the lodge. "Now that we're rid of that horned howler, let's go to sleep."

"Yes, there's a great deal to think upon." De Vaca gazed thoughtfully from Chakoh to the grinning Esteban, shook his head, then sought the comfort of his robes.

Carefully Chakoh gathered the bits of leaves he'd used to make the magic drawing. He carried them outside and buried them before the sun rose. Then he crouched beside Esteban, hugged his knees to his chest, and happily watched his friend soften the dried meat with steady chewing. Esteban was cured and the magic circle of medicine leaves had done it.

Soon his head nodded. He toppled over sound asleep. He woke late in the afternoon.

"No sleep again tonight," Dorantes was grumbling. "It'll be drums and screeching all night long."

"The feast is in our honor," said Cabeza de Vaca. "We must go."

"Why are they suddenly so sure that Esteban will live?"

"Probably because we called in their medicine man. Listen! He's outside speaking to them now."

When the medicine man finished his speech, Chakoh raised the flap and Esteban ducked through. Silence, then a rising hum that ceased when Esteban began to talk in sign language. He gave equal credit for the cure to the Señors and the Buffalo medicine man. The crowd yelled, drums beat, the fire leaped high, and the feast began.

Sitting for long hours with only a scrap of deerskin between himself and the damp ground reminded Chakoh of Esteban's promise. But when he suggested asking the Buffalo People for a deerskin, Esteban shook his head.

"No, little one. When two people wish to trade, each must have something the other wants or needs. These people have everything."

Chakoh nodded sadly. "That is true."

"It is a good life. If it were not for the honors that will surely come to me in Mexico, I would be tempted to stay here."

The thought that Esteban might stay behind stunned Chakoh. The long journey would be unbearable without his friend. He frowned in his effort to chase down a reason to keep Esteban with them.

"You are no medicine man," he said at last.

"To be sure."

"And you cannot hunt the buffalo."

"That is true."

"Then what would you do in this camp?" Chakoh glanced sideways at his friend and added slyly, "To be welcome you must have something the Buffalo People need."

Esteban grinned. "There is always a need for laughter."

"Laughter?"

"To be sure. One cannot use it for trade, but the gift of laughter can make one the companion of kings. I will show you."

At that moment the drums were silent and the circle around the fire clear of dancers. Esteban strode into the center and raised his arms for attention. The Indians watched curiously as he strode around the circle to stop before the medicine man.

"A thousand pardons." He whisked away the medicine man's buffalo robe.

Chakoh tensed at the angry murmur, but Esteban returned to the fire and calmly draped the blanket over his left shoulder. With signs and the few words he'd already learned of the language, Esteban told them, "I am the mighty buffalo hunter."

He swung his shoulders arrogantly and pranced around the fire. Then he dropped the robe, ran to the other side of the circle and put his hands alongside his head, forefingers raised and curved like horns. He snorted and pawed as he had that day long ago in Chakoh's village when he'd imitated a bull and Chakoh had thought of the buffalo. The Indians also recognized the buffalo and leaned forward expectantly, eyes bright in the firelight.

Esteban played both parts, switching so quickly and expertly from hunter to buffalo that Chakoh forgot there was only one man in the circle. The "hunter" waved the robe to tease the "buffalo," skipping lightly away from its charge and mocking it with a stone knife. As the pantomime continued Chakoh found himself cheering with the Indians each time the "buffalo" eluded the deadly swipe of the knife. When the knife at last sliced downward and the "buffalo" rolled over on the hard packed ground, a low moan rose from the circle of watchers. Chakoh almost hated Esteban when the "hunter" pranced about with the robe over his shoulders, bowing and waving.

Then Esteban dropped the robe. Once more all eyes were on the "buffalo" stretched on the ground. The animal's feet stirred. The head lifted and the eyes rolled white in the dancing light. Slowly the "buffalo" rose. Grinning slyly, it trotted tip-toe around the circle, pawed at the ground, and then swiped upward with the right "horn."

Again the "hunter," Esteban bowed and waved. Suddenly he screeched and raced around the circle clutching his rear, his stomach thrown forward at each jump as if avoiding the jabbing horns of the buffalo. He broke through the circle of howling Indians. Chakoh jumped to his feet. He could all but see the maddened buffalo chasing the big man around the teepees.

When the shouts of laughter had faded, Esteban crept up behind Chakoh and lowered himself to the ground.

The Buffalo medicine man rose, retrieved his robe from the ground, and beckoned Esteban once more to the fire. Chakoh leaned forward watching every hand movement and straining to understand the old Indian's meaning.

"I was an old man, weary with the chanting. You fought the buffalo. Tears of laughter washed away the weariness. Now I am young and fresh as new grass after a spring rain. Truly your medicine is great."

With both hands he presented Esteban with a gourd rattle trimmed with red and white feathers and bells made of the tips of deer hoofs.

"For Man-Chased-by-Buffalo."

Esteban bowed his massive head. "A thousand thanks."

When he returned to his place beside Chakoh, his eyes glistened with tears.

Chakoh gazed longingly at the rattle. "It must be strong medicine."

"Very strong." Esteban grinned and cut one of the deer-hoof bells from its thong. "But I do not think this is too powerful for a young boy."

"A thousand thanks." Chakoh placed it gently in his medicine bag. Already he felt the strength of the Buffalo People flowing through him.

The Spaniards were also excited by the gourd rattle.

"We've seen no sign of farming, yet it must have been raised as a crop. They don't grow wild," said Cabeza de Vaca. "Ask where it came from."

The gourds, said the Buffalo People, came down the river with the floods. The spirits sent them for the medicine men. Some years there were many. Some years there were none.

Cabeza de Vaca gazed thoughtfully north, up the river. Chakoh read his look correctly. In the morning the Spaniard announced it was time to move on.

"Then you'll go by yourself," said Dorantes. "Castillo and I have decided to stay."

"Is this true, Castillo?"

The frail Spaniard nodded without breaking his morning prayers. Cabeza de Vaca's beard jutted forward.

"We must go on to Mexico."

"Then go, but I don't intend to risk my neck anymore. The people here are friendly now. Life here is more comfortable than any we've found in years. It is better to stay here than risk death by continuing."

"You must go with me."

Dorantes' mouth lifted in a sneer. "Why?"

"Because we are all that are left from an expedition of over six hundred men. I believe God protected us for a reason, and it was not so we could spend our lives in a teepee helping the women scrape hides and carry water. No, we have been chosen to bring glory to God and King."

"How?"

"I do not know but, then, the journey is not yet over."

Castillo carefully placed the homemade rosary in his pouch and stood up. "I will go with you."

"Fools," snapped Dorantes. "Go on if you wish. I'm safe for the first time in nearly nine years. I intend to stay that way." He turned to Chakoh. "Say good-bye to Esteban, boy. He stays with me."

But Chakoh was speechless, staring in bewilderment from one to the other. He had no difficulty understanding the words. It was the meaning behind them, the reason for speaking them, that escaped him. Without that, words were but hollow sounds.

Cabeza de Vaca walked over and spoke softly to Esteban. "It is up to you. He won't stay if you go."

Esteban passed the rattle nervously from hand to hand. "He ordered me to stay."

"He cannot stop you if you decide to go." Cabeza de Vaca nodded to the group of Buffalo People waiting to accompany them on their journey. They had not hesitated when Esteban asked for guides. "Do you think they will permit Dorantes to harm the Man-Chased-by-Buffalo?"

"There is Mexico."

"I will be there."

Esteban shuffled undecidedly. Chakoh held his breath, trying to read his friend's face. What fun were the fiestas and bullfights of Mexico without Esteban's booming laugh? How would he understand the strange sights without Esteban to explain? For no one else understood his questions. Only yesterday Esteban had said he'd like to spend the rest of his days with this camp. Anxiously Chakoh waited until he saw his friend's familiar grin.

"The sun climbs high." Esteban shook the rattle and pranced to the waiting guides. "Let us be off, my friends."

"Come back here," shouted Dorantes. "Esteban, I forbid you to leave."

But Esteban was already leading the Spaniards through the village. Chakoh trotted by his side, stumbling as he turned to watch Dorantes shriek and shake his fist.

"Does he follow?" asked Esteban.

"No. . . . Yes, he is coming."

Esteban didn't look happy about it. He sighed heavily. "To be sure, I must remember to treat Don Dorantes with care from now on."

"Why?"

"Because Dorantes will be giving a great deal of thought to what *my* treatment will be when we reach Mexico."

"But you know what that will be. You said you would all be welcomed as great warriors. And Dorantes is so weak in spirit you have nothing to fear from him."

Esteban's grin returned. "To be sure, little one. How could I have forgotten? We are doing what no man has done before." He jigged a few steps in time to his rattle. "Come, we are off to Mexico."

Once more Chakoh turned his weary feet along the end-less rim of the world. But their days of hunger were over. The Buffalo People had plenty. At each new village gifts of robes and food were heaped upon the travelers. Often the teepees were emptied of everything the villagers pos-sessed. These gifts the Spaniards gave to their guides, who then returned to their own village. Men from the new village guided them to the next, where the gift-giving cere-mony was repeated. And each set of guides told the new villagers of the Man-Chased-by-Buffalo. Over and over Esteban performed his pantomime.

"To be sure," he told Chakoh, "I am going to be amazed to find a bull instead of a buffalo in the ring in Mexico."

"You mean that is the way you fight the bulls?"

"No, the bulls are fought from horseback."

"Horseback?" Chakoh frowned.

"A horse is something like a deer, but big." Esteban held up his hand to show the height. "Men ride on the horse's back."

Chakoh turned away in disgust. "You never lied to me before, Esteban."

"And I do not lie now. You will see horses and the men who ride them."

"To be sure?"

Esteban laughed. "Yes, little one. To be sure."

They crossed cool pine-covered mountains and turned south at last into dry country dotted with weird-armed cactus. The Buffalo People pointed the way along a river and turned back to their own lands. Their villages were moving to hunt the buffalo. They had already strayed far beyond their usual hunting grounds. They would go no farther.

The Spaniards were not worried. They had only to follow the river. Castillo had recovered his strength and though Dorantes grumbled and scowled incessantly, especially at Esteban, they rationed their food for a week's travel. In three days they found a hunting camp, and the Spaniards marveled at the food the short brown hunters offered.

"Cornmeal," they exclaimed, letting the coarse meal run through their fingers. "Where did it come from? What people are these? Where are their farms?"

Again Chakoh and Esteban settled for long nights beside the campfire learning another tongue.

They called themselves the River People; the Spaniards called them *Pima;* to Chakoh they were the People of Earth Medicine. Never had he seen anything so wonderful and full of mystery.

The Pima planted seeds, sang their medicine songs; and strange plants grew to provide them with corn, beans, squash, and a soft white fluff that the men spun into thread and then wove into loincloths. Surely this was one of Don Castillo's "miracles."

Cabeza de Vaca assured him no magic was needed. If

crops were planted and properly cared for, they provided a harvest. The Spaniards grew many things for food.

Chakoh listened politely, his eyes on Castillo's clicking seed rosary. Surely the chants Castillo murmured to his god had much to do with the growing of food. Such a great thing could not be done without strong medicine, no matter what the Spaniards said. Very well, if the Señors did not wish to teach him their medicine, he would learn that of the Pima. But somehow he must learn this greatest of all magic—growing food.

SIX ✳ A PROFIT IN SCARECROWS

The shelter was open on all four sides to the desert breeze. A roof of long thin sticks provided shade where the family could work or sleep comfortably during the heat of the day. Chakoh sat crosslegged, his fingers working clumsily with the yucca fiber. Esteban sprawled beside him. On the other side an old Pima woman skillfully stitched a round flat basket. From time to time she leaned over to correct Chakoh's work and sigh over his uneven stitches.

This was the largest and most prosperous village they'd

found in their travel through the Pima country. It was also the quietest, for most of the people were sick. The Señors had been working day and night to help break the strange fever.

Castillo came under the shelter and dipped a gourd into the water jar.

"How goes it?" Esteban asked.

"It goes well. There have been no new cases since yesterday morning. Most of the people will be out in the sun tomorrow."

"Go with God," murmured Esteban as the Spaniard hurried off.

Chakoh repeated the words with a sigh. He was glad the Pima were recovering, but he'd be sorry to move on. During their stay he'd learned only enough to make him want to know more about these wonderful people. They were much like the Avavares. Even their winter houses were much the same, but the Pima knew so many more things.

He measured the string sandal against the sole of his foot.

"It is large enough now. Will you show me again how to finish it, Aunt Maria?"

The Pima would not speak their own names. The Spaniards had given them Spanish ones and Esteban had taken to calling the stout woman they lived with Aunt Maria. Chakoh did the same.

Maria showed Chakoh how to weave in the loose end of the fine yucca and fasten the tie strings. "Sandal making is woman's work."

"But there is no woman with us to learn, Aunt Maria." It was strange that the Avavares wove so many mats for houses but had never thought of making sandals. "The next pair will be for Don Castillo. He needs them most. I would like to make a pair for each of us, but we won't be here long enough."

Esteban lifted his enormous foot. "A great disappointment. I thought to have some protection for my dainty feet."

The Indian woman's eyes twinkled. "That is no problem, Dark One. I have two empty storage baskets that will fit you nicely."

Chakoh grinned and stretched his fingers. The sun was not yet overhead. Men still hoed young corn along the irrigation ditches. In other fields young boys chased thieving birds from the precious hills of corn and beans.

Suddenly Esteban sat up and chuckled. "Little One, do you remember the new loincloth I promised you?"

"My skin has grown so tough I no longer need it."

"Nevertheless, I promised and you shall have it."

Chakoh dropped the half-finished sandal and tagged along curious to see what Esteban had to trade. These Pima needed even less than the Buffalo People. When he discovered that Esteban was only picking up sticks and begging bits of rabbit fur from the women, Chakoh returned to his sandal making.

Either Esteban was joking or he'd lost his senses. Perhaps he'd caught the fever. Chakoh quickly made the sign of the Señors in the air. But Esteban was down by the irrigation ditches, and Chakoh doubted it would have any effect at that distance. However, he had plenty of the dried tea leaves and a bell from the Buffalo People. If the Spirit-of-Misfortune breathed on Esteban, Chakoh could make medicine again.

He was so busy planning the ritual that he didn't notice the cries and shouts until Aunt Maria clapped her hands.

"Look what the Dark One made."

A stick had been driven into the center of a field. Another stick had been tied across it near the top. From this second stick fluttered bits of cloth and fur. On top of the first stick Esteban impaled a squash with stones pounded in place for eyes and grinning mouth.

Aunt Maria ducked into the winter home and came out with bits of deerskin and cloth. She pushed them into Chakoh's hands.

"Ask him to make one for my husband's field. Tell him I will pay well."

Chakoh pushed his way through the crowd to where Esteban stood scratching his head. "What is it, Esteban?"

"It's just a makeshift scarecrow. I thought to trade a few

of them for a loincloth, but these men believe it's some sort of charm or magic for their corn."

"Aunt Maria wants one for her husband's field. She said she would pay you well."

"So say they all."

Early in the trading Esteban received a length of the wonderful cotton cloth, which he gave to Chakoh. Chakoh then donated his old deerskin loincloth for the making of more scarecrows. By sundown each field had its own gourd-head charm. Esteban had baskets, rattles to tie around his knees, feathers for his hair, and two blue stones he called turquoise.

"Would you do a favor for me, little one?"

"To be sure. I'm grateful for the chance to do something for you." Chakoh's hands smoothed the soft white loin-cloth. Not even the chewed deerskin of the Buffalo People was so fine and soft.

"Would you keep these blue stones for me until we reach Mexico?"

Chakoh placed the stones carefully in his medicine bag. They looked like bits of sky against the dark dried leaves.

"And say nothing of them to the Señors," Esteban added.

"Why not?" Nothing was ever kept from the Spaniards.

Esteban scratched his head. "It is hard to explain, but such things as turquoise and gold have a strange effect upon the gentlest of Spaniards."

"You mean they are bad medicine?"

"Only to the Spaniards. They will not harm you, little one. For you the blue stones are good medicine."

Chakoh nodded wisely. He knew well the strange and mysterious ways of medicine, good and bad. But their caution was wasted. The Spaniards were waiting for them at Aunt Maria's. In Dorantes' outstretched hand lay seven blue stones and three green arrowheads.

"Look at these," he shouted. "Turquoise and emeralds. Quickly, Esteban. Ask where they came from."

Though the Spaniards had learned a few words of the Pima tongue, they insisted that Esteban translate the questions and answers so there'd be no misunderstanding. It took a long time to collect Aunt Maria's information.

The stones and arrowheads came from the north, from a very strange and unfriendly people. It was too bad the Spaniards had not arrived sooner. Just before planting time some of those people had passed through this very village on their way south to trade the blue stones for parrot feathers. No, they did not make the journey often. Only twice could Maria remember them passing through the village, and only once had her husband traveled to their land to trade. That was long ago, when he was young enough to endure the long, dangerous trip.

"Where's her husband?" said Dorantes. "Let us question him."

It would be a clear moonlit night. Her husband was

preparing to sing to the growing corn. He could not be disturbed.

"But he has told of the trip so often," said Maria, "that it is as if I'd made it myself. I can tell you all you wish to know."

Yes, the people to the north were very wealthy, but they used their precious stones and feathers to make horrible ceremonial masks. It was a good place for strangers to avoid.

The Spaniards chattered excitedly about the Aztecs and their masks of gold. This land might be another Mexico. Maria's next bit of information convinced them.

These people lived in great solid houses, one house atop another, four or five houses high. Many of these houses were walled together in great cities. Seven cities, she believed her husband had said. The Pima called the place Cíbola.

"Cíbola!" Cabeza de Vaca crossed himself. "By the grace of God, we've discovered the seven golden cities of Antilia. They must be the same."

"It is for this that God spared our lives," said Castillo.

Dorantes said impatiently, "No more delay. We must get to Mexico immediately. The Viceroy must be told at once and someone should go to Spain and petition the King for command of an expedition. Perhaps Castillo and I can . . ."

"That can wait until we get to Mexico," said Cabeza de

Vaca. "We leave before dawn."

In the morning Aunt Maria wept and begged Chakoh to stay with her.

"All my daughters have married and gone to live with their husbands' families. That is as it should be, but we are lonely. Never have we had a son. You will be like our own, Chakoh."

He hesitated. He hadn't yet learned the songs that Aunt Maria's husband sang to the corn. He knew there was a planting song, one to be sung when the corn sprouted, another when it tasseled, and the most important when the ears began to form. Aunt Maria had explained the harvesting, parching, and storing; but what good was that knowledge if one hadn't the medicine to grow the corn? There was also the magic of spinning and weaving. So much he could learn from the Pima if he stayed.

He turned to Esteban. "And you, will you stay also?"

"No, little one. There will be honor and glory for those who bring news of the Seven Cities. But when the Viceroy hears of the wealth of Cíbola, we will surely be retracing our steps."

"I will return," Chakoh promised the tearful woman. Then he followed the dancing, jingling, singing Esteban. Twenty of the villagers, loaded with food for the journey, followed more slowly with the Spaniards.

The journey went well for several days. At every village

more people joined them. Others traveled great distances to see or be healed by the Señors. Then they reached a river too flooded to cross and camped fifteen days on its banks. It was there that Chakoh saw the evil medicine of the blue stones working in the Señors.

Cabeza de Vaca was more silent than ever. Dorantes no longer spoke to de Vaca at all but sent messages through Esteban, even though the two Spaniards shared the same cookfire. Most astonishing of all, Castillo no longer fingered his prayer beads but huddled with Dorantes. Together they drew numbers in the dirt, argued, erased the symbols and figured again. On the fifth day they quarreled over who would be governor of Cíbola.

"Now no one is speaking to anyone," said Chakoh. "Is this the medicine of the blue stones?"

"To be sure," said Esteban. "It is part of the magic of Cíbola."

After that he kept Chakoh away from the camp. They fashioned bark boats and sent them floating down the rapids. Together they raced along the shore, leaping brush and watersoaked logs, cheering their boats to the goal they'd chosen. When Chakoh's boat snagged or capsized, Esteban's laughter shook the trees; but when his own boat lost, he laughed even louder. Chakoh was sorry to see the river drain, because the journey would continue. It had been a fine time in spite of the quarrels.

"Never mind," said Esteban. "There will be better times in Mexico."

In the seventh village after the river Castillo discovered an Indian wearing a strange charm around his neck. Esteban explained it was a buckle from a Spanish sword belt, with a horseshoe nail fastened to it. So Esteban had not lied. There were such beasts as horses. When asked where he had gotten his charm, the man pointed to the southwest.

"But do not go there," he warned. "Those hair-faces are evil."

"They are our people," said Cabeza de Vaca.

"They cannot be your people. You came from the rising sun. They came from the other way. You have healed our sick and our quarrels. They bring us death and slavery. You ask for nothing and give freely whatever you have. They take everything they see."

Chakoh snorted in disgust. What did these people expect? Instead of fighting like true warriors, they ran and hid in the mountains. Such cowards received what they deserved.

Cabeza de Vaca did not agree.

"Those evil hair-faces are few," he said. "I will have them punished when I see the Viceroy. The raiding will stop, but if hair-faces should come again before I reach my people, give this sign and they will not harm you."

He touched fingers to forehead, chest, and shoulders.

The Indians repeated it solemnly. But it did not calm their fears for the Señors.

"Stay with us," they pleaded. "You are safe here."

The Spaniards refused and hurried on. They descended to a valley better watered, with larger, richer fields than those of Aunt Maria's village, but the fields had been trampled by great animals. Chakoh had never seen such tracks before. The huts were deserted. Many had been burned.

"The slave raiders," muttered Esteban. "To be sure, we are near Mexico."

His angry strides lengthened so that Chakoh had to trot to keep up.

"What is the matter, Esteban?" He had never seen such anger in his friend's face.

"Ten years is a long time. When one walks the earth's rim one forgets the pattern on the other side of the basket. Perhaps we should have stayed with Aunt Maria." After a moment he added quietly, "No, it will be different. Cabeza de Vaca promised."

Chakoh nodded. "And he gave the Indians the magic sign for protection."

"That is not what I meant."

He would explain no further. While Chakoh puzzled over Esteban's words Cabeza de Vaca shouted and rushed ahead. Four horsemen rode to meet him. The Spanish soldiers wore shining breastplates and headpieces with plumes.

Their powerful beasts, larger than any deer, reared and pawed, but the riders forced them to obey with only a thin rope.

Chakoh edged behind Esteban. Surely he would know the mysteries of controlling these beasts, should one attack.

The soldiers listened in amazement to Cabeza de Vaca's story.

"But the Narváez expedition perished ten years ago in Florida. You can't be de Vaca. It's impossible!"

"But true, my friend."

They were taken to the settlement of Culiacán. The fields stretched as far as Chakoh could see, but the crops were not nearly so strange as the sheep and cattle grazing in the fields. The buildings were enormous. Each room was larger than any hut or teepee Chakoh had ever seen.

"Is this Mexico?" he wondered.

Esteban laughed. "No, little one. This is only the home of Señor Diaz."

"You mean that Mexico is larger?"

"A hundred times larger with as many more people."

Chakoh shivered. "I think I would rather hunt the buffalo. I did not know the Spaniards were so powerful."

"Don't worry, little one. I will be with you."

But his worry mounted as they followed their escort of soldiers, each day's journey bringing them nearer to the home of the unknown god.

SEVEN ✳ MEXICO

Mexico! With all the tongues he'd learned, Chakoh still had no words to describe its wonders. The city was set in the middle of a lake with wide roads spanning the water. Houses of brightly painted clay bricks lined the canals and streets. People of all kinds jostled against each other in the Plaza, where merchants shouted for all to come purchase their wares. Two eyes could not see all its marvels, though the noise and stench made Chakoh wish for the open desert.

They turned off the Plaza into a narrow street and halted before the high walls of the Mercederian abbey. While Cabeza de Vaca went inside to arrange Chakoh's care the boy said his farewells to Esteban.

"I will see you soon?"

"To be sure. As soon as we finish our report at the Viceroy's palace."

"Go with God." Chakoh watched the shabby procession force its way through the market place, Esteban's dark head towering over everyone.

"Welcome." A stout man in a long brown robe embraced Chakoh and led him into the walled garden.

"Are you a priest?" asked Chakoh.

The man laughed. "Not I. I am only Brother Solano, keeper of the kitchen and the kitchen garden."

Hands on hips, Brother Solano proudly surveyed his domain. Three other brown-robed men worked among neat rows of vegetables, fruit trees, and grape vines trained along the garden wall.

"Are all these things good to eat?" asked Chakoh.

"Certainly. Or they will be someday. The fruit trees have just begun to bear, all except for the oranges. We lost the first ones brought from Spain but I have great hopes for these, if it please God." He crossed himself, then peered closely at Chakoh's face. "Are you hungry, lad?"

Chakoh nodded.

"Why didn't you speak up? Come along."

Though heavy as a bear before its winter sleep, Brother Solano moved briskly about the kitchen from fireplace spit to storage baskets to thick clay jars. One wooden bowl after another appeared on the table. Brother Solano's tongue worked as rapidly as his hands.

"Nothing gives the Lord more pleasure than to see the fruits of His earth eaten with joy and appreciation. The goose has much longer to cook for the evening meal, but thanks to someone forgetting to turn the spit, a few slices from this side will do nicely."

He plunged a pudgy finger into a bowl, licked it, nodded, and set the bowl before Chakoh. "The tortillas are cold but the chili is hot enough." He made Chakoh wait until he'd offered a prayer of thanksgiving, then ordered: "Eat, lad, and praise God for His bounteous fruits. Ah! I forgot."

Brother Solano turned to the open door. "Brother Garcia, are there ripe apricots on that tree in the corner? We have a guest."

As he ate, Chakoh gazed through the open door at the brothers working in the green garden. At the waist of each brown robe swung prayer beads like Don Castillo's. No matter what the Señors said, Chakoh was certain those beads were the secret of growing things. Hadn't Brother Solano just said everything in the garden belonged to God?

Another brother poked his bald head into the kitchen. "Fray Marcos wants the boy."

"All in good time," said Brother Solano. "Give the lad time to eat. How can one contemplate God's word if an empty stomach keeps interrupting one's thoughts?"

With a bit of tortilla Chakoh scooped up a last mouthful of chili and gulped it down. He stared longingly at the other dishes but said, "I am ready to go now."

He'd come to Mexico to learn of the new god so he could save his people from the Spirit-of-Misfortune. That was more important than food. He sighed.

Brother Solano grumbled. "Rushing the lad through his meal. He's hardly eaten enough to last him through vespers. Here, lad, take these."

He pressed two round cakes into Chakoh's hand.

"What are they?"

"Yam cakes sweetened with honey and flavored with vanilla and lime." He grinned at Chakoh's delight. "Here, take two more. Ah, it's a pleasure to have someone who enjoys his food."

"A thousand thanks," murmured Chakoh shyly and then followed the hairless brother down a long corridor. He marveled at the smooth stone floor beneath his sandals, the cloth draping the walls, and the heavy carved furniture in every room. He wondered if he'd be able to find his way back to the kitchen.

The brother pushed him gently through still another

door. A thin hollow-cheeked man in a coarse gray robe beckoned Chakoh to step forward.

"I am Fray Marcos de Niza. Cabeza de Vaca tells me you speak Spanish."

Chakoh nodded. This was the man who made medicine to the powerful Spanish god. Did he dare speak aloud? Yet the priest did not look too different from the three Señors. Except for his eyes. They burned with a fierceness Chakoh had seen only twice: first when Cabeza de Vaca had urged Dorantes and Castillo to leave the Buffalo People and then when they'd heard of Cíbola.

"Sit down, my son."

Chakoh shifted his feet uneasily.

"On the floor if you wish."

But Chakoh edged his rump gingerly onto the edge of a high-backed chair, fearful that it would collapse under him. However, he was in Mexico now. He must learn new ways.

"Now tell me of your own people and of all those you met on your journey."

Chakoh was disappointed. He'd thought Fray Marcos was going to teach him the mysteries of the new god; but he obediently told of his home, the tea drinkers, the Buffalo People, and Aunt Maria's village. The chair seat cut into the backs of his legs. He wriggled his toes to keep feeling in them. In spite of Brother Solano's assurances that a full stomach was best for thinking, Chakoh felt groggy from the heavy meal. Only by great effort could he keep his mind on the trail he'd traveled with Esteban and the three Señors.

Question followed question until a bell pealed nearby.

"Vespers," said Fray Marcos. "Will you come to the church?"

Wide-awake, Chakoh jumped eagerly to his feet. At last he would see this wondrous cave where the Spanish god lived.

It was not as he had imagined. There were no villages, no moon nor sun inside the pink stone building, but its soaring vastness filled him with as much wonder as did the flickering candles. And surely only a god could have formed the many statues and the ornate carved pillars.

"What a great place," murmured Chakoh. "It is so large the top and sides are lost in the shadows."

Fray Marcos smiled. When the evening prayers were over, he led Chakoh outside and showed him the great cathedral being built across the Plaza. Though the light was failing, Indian slaves still labored with the great stone blocks salvaged from the Aztec temple that had once stood on that very spot. They plodded listlessly, dragging their heavy loads.

"Do they never try to escape?" asked Chakoh.

"Sometimes, but they are always returned. They cannot hide with such a mark."

Chakoh moved closer to the shuffling line of slaves. In

the twilight he could barely see the large S branded on their right cheek, but in daylight there would be no way to hide it.

Could these be the Aztecs that Cortez had conquered? No, they couldn't be. Esteban had said the Aztecs were valiant fighters. Courageous warriors never allowed themselves to be taken into slavery. These must be from another tribe of small spirit and no sense of shame. But hadn't Esteban also said the Aztecs had surrendered rather than starve in their lake city? If so, they deserved to wear their shame where everyone could see. He turned away in disgust, but the memory of the slow shuffling men lurked in the corner of his mind and made him uneasy.

Back at the abbey he slipped away from Fray Marcos and found his way to the kitchen. The brothers rushed about, while Brother Solano shouted instructions only to push aside each helper and perform the task himself.

"Here, serve the fathers and get out from underfoot." Brother Solano ladened everyone with glazed green dishes and wooden bowls, then shooed them out of the room. Chakoh huddled quietly in the corner hoping he wouldn't be noticed and shouted at. But nothing in his kitchen escaped Brother Solano.

"Don't stand there, lad. Sit here on the bench and eat."

The food that passed endlessly before him was all that Esteban had said. There were tortillas, beans, goose, bacon, strange juicy fruits, yam cakes, and cup after cup of foaming chocolate. When Chakoh could not force another mouthful past his lips, the portly brother still urged him to eat.

"Come, lad. You have no padding on your bones."

"I have more than Fray Marcos."

"Ah, him." Brother Solano snorted. "He thinks nothing of his stomach. I could serve him burned sandals without salt and he wouldn't know the difference. In truth, I do not think he would eat at all if someone didn't remind him."

Chakoh remembered the long fasts of the medicine men. "He must be a great priest."

"No doubt. I have heard he did great things in Peru with Pizarro, but such things are too far beyond my kitchen. Have more yam cakes. The good Lord was generous with the crop this year."

Brother Solano crossed himself in thanksgiving.

Before Chakoh could ask about the garden, he was once again summoned to Fray Marcos de Niza.

"The Viceroy has sent instructions for your care and training. There is also a bundle of clothes, but first you must be baptized."

After many questions and instructions Chakoh was led into a small chapel. There in the flickering light of the wondrous candles Chakoh's head was sprinkled with water. He was given a new name, Juan, to please the Spanish god. With that small ceremony his whole life changed.

One marvel treaded fast upon the heels of another. His red-curtained bed was a sleeping teepee inside a room larger than two huts. On one of the bed posts he hung his bow and quiver. Tenderly he laid the breechcloth Esteban had given him in the bottom of an empty carved chest. He sighed as the lid dropped over it with a thud. He would not miss its comfort so much if he could wear the long robes and sandals of the brothers, but Fray Marcos said that was impossible. The Viceroy had provided his clothes. Chakoh must wear them.

Tying the long stockings to the string around his waist took more time than morning prayers. The starched neck ruff scratched him raw, but there was room inside the slashed, stiffened breeches to hide the precious medicine bag. For weeks he walked straddle-legged, forever tugging and pulling his clothes in a futile effort to ease his discomfort, but at last his body adjusted itself to its new covering just as Chakoh became accustomed to his new life.

The day began before dawn, with kneeling on the stone floor of the church as a priest sang mass in a deep thrilling voice. After a small meal there were lessons from Fray Marcos. Chakoh listened closely. The prayers and rituals were most important, but the lessons drained from his mind like water through a basket. Enough caught in the crevices for him to follow mass and stumble through the shorter prayers, but there was so much new and wonderful that his brain could not hold it all. Besides there was always the nagging ache of Esteban's broken promise, for the weeks passed and he still did not return.

Chakoh knew the report had been made long ago to the Viceroy, for the marketplace buzzed with tales of the Seven Cities of Cíbola. It was larger than Mexico, richer than Peru. It was whispered that the people of Cíbola used sweat scrapers of pure gold and hunted even common rabbits with emerald arrowheads. Though Chakoh never saw the three Señors, he heard rumors of their ignored petitions to the Viceroy and their plans to return to Spain. By constant questioning he learned only one thing for certain. Esteban was not with any of the Señors. He had not only vanished, so far as Mexico was concerned, he had never existed.

But the two blue stones in the medicine bag bouncing inside his breeches were real. Chakoh never knelt on the stone floor for mass that he did not search the church for the curly black head. Whenever errands took him through the Plaza, he watched for the familiar broad shoulders.

He will come, Chakoh told himself over and over. He promised, and Esteban has never broken his word. He will come.

But summer grew old and passed away, and Esteban did not come. Cold winds swept down from the smoking snow-capped mountains. Chakoh was comfortable under a new short cloak, for winter in Mexico lacked the freezing north winds, the sleet, and snow of his homeland. If only cloak or sun or Brother Solano's kitchen fire could warm the cold fear in his heart. For Chakoh was sure Esteban was dead. Nothing else would have kept him away. He resolved never again to look at the white loincloth in the chest, but for some reason he could not explain even to himself he continued to hide the medicine bag with the blue stones beneath his breeches.

Esteban's fate was not the only cause of his fear. Comfort had faded his recollection of his own country. At night in the snug warmth of his curtained bed, Chakoh assembled piece by piece a picture of mountains, canyon, cactus, and catclaw thickets. He was no longer certain that such a country really existed. Perhaps he'd created it in his mind. Surely no country could be so harsh and cruel. Then the faces of his parents came sharp and clear. With them came also the memory of the wretched starving village. Hunger was one thing he would never forget. Another was Esteban.

Without him Mexico was a lonely place. Fray Marcos taught him, Brother Solano fed him; but there was little laughter and no one to whom he could speak of the things that troubled his heart.

His lessons grew shorter. He'd at last mastered the prayer beads. Fray Marcos was pleased. The priest spoke often of Chakoh's return to his own village and how much he could teach his own people of the ways of God. With that thought, Chakoh's heart squeezed painfully. Was that all there was to be for him, a life of misery and starvation? How could he return to his own land after seeing Mexico?

If only Esteban were here. *To be sure, little one,* he would say, *Mexico is the greatest place on the rim of the earth. To be sure, you must remain here always.* That is what he would say. Or would he? The lonely days and the long nights brought no answer.

The celebration of the birth of Christ pushed the doubts from his mind. The processions were unlike anything Chakoh had ever seen. The people were happy, the city bright and gay. Then came the fiesta and the Plaza thronged with people, all eager for the bullfight that followed. For a moment Chakoh's heart leaped. He pushed his way around the Plaza searching for the tall dark man that had promised to take him to the bullfight. As always, his search ended in disappointment. Esteban was nowhere in the square. Surely he was dead.

The crowd surged toward the gates. The trumpets sounded. Chakoh hesitated, but what were the bullfights without Esteban's laughter and foolish talk? He trudged back to his silent room.

The days dragged by, then a softening of the morning air reminded him that spring, the time for travel, was not far away. The questions returned with renewed urgency. In desperation Chakoh sought the comfort of Brother Solano's kitchen, but the cook was no help.

"Such things are beyond me," he said. "Have a yam cake."

Chakoh accepted it with a sigh. "If only I could talk to Esteban again. He'd know if I should stay."

"Him again." Brother Solano shook his head over the tortilla he was patting into shape. "You speak of that man as if he were Saint James himself."

"Esteban was the wisest, bravest man there ever was. Did I tell you how he saved me from the tea drinkers?"

"Many times. Here, have a dried fig. You are eating even less than Fray Marcos these days."

"Fray Marcos is seldom here these days," Chakoh reminded him. "He spends most of his time at the Viceroy's palace."

There was no reply. Chakoh hinted again. "It must be a matter of great importance that keeps him there."

"No doubt. But I know nothing of such affairs. I do know that I need salt."

Chakoh leaned forward to peer into the clay jar, but the cook snatched it away from his view.

"This is my kitchen and when I say I need salt for the main meal, I need salt," he thundered. In a softer tone he added, "And there's no need for you to hurry. Take time to talk. Enjoy yourself. I know how much you like the market."

That had been true before the loneliness and doubts

had begun gnawing at him. Today Chakoh wandered list-lessly between the stalls and mats, hardly glancing at the wares spread for inspection, and not stopping to enjoy the haggling and good-natured name-calling that preceded each purchase.

The tales of fabulous Cíbola had grown with the winter. It was no secret that the Viceroy was organizing a great expedition. All around Chakoh, men talked of the great army and wondered who would command it.

"Look there," said a wine merchant. "Old Cortez himself."

"What could have brought him into the city?" wondered a bystander.

The wine merchant, a retired soldier, glared at him. "The Viceroy wants him to command the expedition to Cíbola, of course."

"The Viceroy favors that Coronado. Old man Cortez has just come in to beg again."

The voices rose to fighting pitch as Chakoh pushed his way toward the palace. He reached the ornate iron gates in time to watch the horseman approach through the gathering crowd. Chakoh gazed up into sad eyes. An old scar showed through the black beard liberally streaked with gray. The great conqueror had grown old and weary, but he was still the great Cortez of Esteban's stories. Chakoh was awestruck when Cortez dismounted and handed him the reins.

"See that he's well cared for."

"But—but . . ." Chakoh tried to explain he was not a court page in spite of his clothes, but the words wouldn't come until the broad back had disappeared inside the courtyard.

Chakoh stared fearfully at the great beast on the other end of the frail leather straps, then glanced about for someone to whom he could hand the reins. The crowd was already drifting away in search of other excitement. He would have to take this monster to the stable himself.

Never before had he been so close to a horse. He was sure the large dark eyes glinted with wickedness, only waiting for him to turn his back. His left arm stretched full length and clutching the very end of the reins, Chakoh stepped slowly backward. The horse followed. Feeling the wall with his right hand Chakoh slowly led the animal around the corner toward the carriage gates. Chakoh wrinkled his nose at the smell of the stables, but the horse stepped forward eagerly. Chakoh hurried backward, but the impatient horse jerked the reins from his hand and trotted into the littered stableyard.

"A thousand thanks," Chakoh whispered and crossed himself.

As he leaned against the gates and waited for his trembling knees to stiffen he watched the activity in the stableyard. He'd always avoided this narrow lane because of the rank smell that was worse here than any other place in

Mexico. Now that he'd been forced to come, he watched curiously as thin Negroes and stooped Indians moved listlessly through their duties.

"You, there," boomed a voice. "Unsaddle that horse."

Chakoh stiffened. Heart pounding he stepped through the gates and searched the side of the yard that had been hidden from his view. A tall familiar figure strode from a pile of hay to direct the feeding of Cortez's horse.

"Esteban!" Chakoh flung himself at his friend.

EIGHT ✳ LORD OF THE VICEROY'S STABLES

"It is the little one, to be sure!" Esteban scooped the boy up in a welcoming hug.

Chakoh scrambled out of the embrace and breathed deeply to be sure no ribs were cracked. "I searched and searched for you. I thought surely you were dead. Before the bullfight I . . . " But what did that matter? Esteban was alive! He rubbed the moisture from his eyes.

"Where have you been?" Chakoh asked.

"Here."

"But why didn't you ... ?"

Esteban grabbed his shoulders and spun him around. "Let me look at you. Ay, yi! Stuffed and laced like a court page. Perhaps I should call you *Don* Chakoh now."

For the first time Chakoh noticed Esteban's rags. He'd heard the three Señors were angry because they'd not received their expected reward from the Viceroy.

"Did the Viceroy refuse your petition too?" he asked.

"What petition?"

All Chakoh knew of petitions was that they were of great value and importance. Everyone spoke of them with longing.

"The honors you expected," he explained. "Didn't you receive them?"

"To be sure." Esteban's laugh was bitter. He waved grandly at the courtyard. "Can't you see? I am now lord of the Viceroy's stables. That is my reward."

Chakoh turned slowly inspecting the horses, carriages, and slaves. Surely Esteban's position must be one of importance, but he was only across the Plaza. Couldn't he have found a few moments to keep his promise?

A hand ruffled his hair. "I would have come if they had let me, little one. You know that, don't you?"

Chakoh sighed and nodded. Fray Marcos had little time for himself, and Esteban was surely even more important.

His duty to the Viceroy came first. Any doubts Chakoh had were banished by the relief and joy of finding Esteban alive.

"I have thought of you often, little one. Now that you are here, tell me what great adventures you've had."

As Chakoh chattered about his lessons and life in the abbey Esteban carried forkfuls of hay in to the stabled horses. Chakoh followed him back and forth. On the third trip he interrupted his story to ask, "Must you do that?"

"To be sure."

Chakoh shrugged and continued to trail behind. "So you see," he finished proudly, "I have learned a great many things."

"One can learn things anywhere. You could have learned a great many things from the Buffalo People also."

"Them," said Chakoh scornfully.

Esteban dropped the hay in front of Cortez's horse, wiped his face on the back of his hand and stared down at Chakoh. "You once thought the buffalo hunters were great people."

"I was foolish and ignorant then."

Esteban grinned.

"It is true," Chakoh continued stubbornly. "Their hide teepees are nothing compared to Mexico. They eat nothing but meat and berries. Here in the market are more kinds of food than there are spots on a fawn."

"That is true, but the Buffalo People would have taught you to hunt the great humped cows. Have you learned how to hunt mutton and tortillas and chocolate?"

"Now it is you who are foolish." Chakoh turned on his heel and stalked to the pile of hay, not waiting for Esteban. "I have learned a great many things," he repeated loudly.

"But the things you would have learned with the Buffalo People would have been useful."

"These things are useful." He kicked at the hay, but it offered no resistance and his anger mounted. Why must Esteban spoil things by saying what Chakoh had no wish to hear?

"Only in Mexico."

"Then I will stay in Mexico," Chakoh shouted.

The words seemed to hang in the air repeating themselves like the peal of bells. Chakoh stared up at his friend and wished the words safely back in his mouth. Never before had he seen that dark face frozen in anger. Fearfully Chakoh edged backward.

"What have they promised you?" The voice was flat and menacing.

"Nothing," he whispered. "They have promised me nothing."

"They will." There was no mirth in Esteban's glittering smile. "To be sure, they will make a great many promises. And they will keep none of them."

Chakoh wanted to deny it, but he was too frightened by

his friend's anger to speak. Esteban stood glaring into space, lost in his thoughts. Chakoh edged away, then hesitated.

"Esteban?" he said softly.

There was no answer. Slowly Chakoh picked his way through the stable litter. He looked back from the gate. Esteban had not moved. Chakoh sighed and moved into the bustling Plaza.

"Salt beef, good salt beef that will not spoil even in the hot country."

"Honey! Who wants honey?"

"Fine mats from Puebla." The mat seller tapped Chakoh's stockinged leg. "Watch your feet, boy."

"Behold this fine parrot that once graced Montezuma's garden. A beautiful bird and bites only a little."

A beggar, mistaking Chakoh for the son of a noble, hobbled pitifully on a crutch and whined for mercy. Chakoh shook his head sadly. The beggar muttered an oath, then spied a captain in shining armor and raced nimbly through the crowd to beg from the soldier.

Chakoh wandered aimlessly through the market. The profusion of goods was as bewildering and the noise as deafening as they'd been the first time he'd seen the Plaza. When he came to the salt seller's, he remembered Brother Solano's order. The salt was measured and tied in a square of cloth. Chakoh knew the salt seller would come to the abbey on a certain day to be paid by the fathers. But suppose he wanted to buy something for himself? What would he do?

Mats could be traded for honey, honey for tortillas, chocolate beans for cotton. But where did one get the mats and honey and cotton? Or the gold that was of even greater value? In spite of himself Esteban's words gnawed at his mind.

He did not have to remain in Mexico. He could go home. Go home to starve. His laugh was as bitter as Esteban's. No, he could never return. As soon as he had said that he would stay in Mexico, he knew it was what he'd intended to do all along. But how did one hunt in Mexico?

He watched the beggars quarreling over a scrap of tortilla. He'd never before noticed there were so many beggars. Was it possible to starve in Mexico? Then he remembered that the "lame" beggar had run swiftly through the market. The man was not really crippled. He didn't have to beg unless, like Chakoh, he did not know the secret of hunting in Mexico.

A coldness settled over Chakoh's heart. Would the same thing happen to him? It was one thing to starve in his own harsh country where there was no food; it would be quite another to starve in the midst of Mexico's plenty. He glanced across the Plaza to the laboring slaves. For a moment he felt understanding for the warriors who must have watched their children starving here on this very Plaza, but a soldier bumped against him. The movement swung the medicine bag against his leg. He remembered the warriors in his own village and his heart hardened. The "lame" beggar had more honor than these branded slaves. In his own way the beggar still fought.

He jumped as a hand touched his shoulder. Fray Marcos smiled down, his dark eyes gleaming.

"The bells are ringing for vespers, my son."

"Yes, Father." He hurried after the priest wondering if it would offend the Spanish god to have a bundle of salt brought into the church. There was no time to take it to the kitchen. He crossed himself and was about to spit over his left shoulder when he saw Fray Marcos looking at him. Chakoh smiled weakly.

"I have just come from the Viceroy," said the priest. "We have great plans for you, my son."

He looked as if he would say more, but they were entering the hushed twilight of the church. Chakoh knelt on the cold stones and thanked the Spanish god and the Spirit-of-Good-Things for whispering the great plans, whatever they were, into the Viceroy's ear. No longer need he worry over Esteban's strange words.

After vespers he hurried to the kitchen.

Brother Solano stared at the bundle Chakoh dropped on the table. "What's this?"

"Salt."

"Salt?"

Chakoh grinned at the cook's confusion. Just as he'd

thought. The errand had been another of Brother Solano's efforts to cheer him. If the yam cakes didn't help, a trip to the market would. For once the cook had been right. On this trip he'd found Esteban. Nothing could make him happier.

When he struggled out of his clothes that night he fingered the medicine bag thoughtfully before hanging it beside the unused bow. In the excitement of seeing Esteban he'd forgotten the blue stones. Tomorrow he would take them to Esteban and pretend their argument had never been. Curled in his bed Chakoh wondered at the placid man's unusual anger. What could have caused it?

"And what does it matter?" he muttered. "Tomorrow it will be forgotten." And he dropped it from his mind as unimportant.

For the first time in months Chakoh stood shivering in the pre-dawn chill, gazing longingly at the wooden chest. If only he could wrap the breechcloth around him and sneak off to meet Esteban. But the steady brush of sandals on the hall floor told him it was impossible. He fought the daily battle with strings and buttons and hurried to mass. Never before had the ritual seemed so long, the floor so hard and the church so cold. He crossed his ankles and sat on them, then uncrossed them and grimaced at the thousand needles in his feet and toes. He raveled loose threads from his breeches and twisted the buttons on his doublet until Fray Marcos' stern eyes shocked the words to the prayers back into his memory.

Brother Solano grumbled over his hasty meal. "You are just like Fray Marcos lately. Food has no meaning for you."

"Your food has," said Chakoh. "It is the best."

"Then why don't you eat it?"

"I am in a great hurry. I must meet Esteban."

"And do you think the great and wonderful Esteban wants you to perish from hunger before his very eyes?"

Chakoh grinned. "I think the great and wonderful Esteban would say your yam cakes were the best in all Mexico. If he could taste them, that is."

Brother Solano filled his hands with the small cakes. "Take them and go. I want no walking skeletons in my kitchen. It is proof of the Lord's goodness that He continues to shower His bounty on the earth in spite of weak appetites."

Chakoh sprinted across the Plaza, heedless of the shouts and threats that followed his headlong passage. He raced around the palace to the large double carriage gates and into the stableyard. The horses were being watered. Slaves staggered across the yard with the large leather buckets of water. Chakoh proudly watched Esteban walking as easily as if his hands were empty.

"How goes it, Esteban?"

Esteban grinned at Chakoh's full hands. "It goes hungry."

As they squatted on their heels and shared the yam cakes Chakoh repeated the cook's words.

"He should have shared our fish bones and lizards," said

Esteban. "Then perhaps he wouldn't praise the Lord's bounty."

"The Lord is a Spanish god. That is why Mexico is so wonderful. His home is here."

"Is that one of the useful things you have learned?"

"No, it is what anyone can see for himself." Couldn't Esteban forget yesterday? Chakoh didn't want to quarrel again.

"And anyone can see for himself that he cannot just sit and let the Lord's bounty fall into his cookpot."

"I don't expect to."

"What will you do?"

"I don't know, but Fray Marcos said only yesterday that he has great plans for me."

"To be sure. He would like you to become a brother or perhaps a priest."

Chakoh thought of Brother Solano's kitchen and grinned. "That would be all right."

"Your feet walk a strange trail, little one. Can you see the end?"

"I walked a strange trail once before. To Mexico." And that time, also, Esteban had warned him not to come. Chakoh frowned. "Why didn't you want me to come to Mexico?"

"You have been here most of a year. You should know."

"I see nothing to fear."

Esteban shook his great head. "Ay, yi, little one! Do you

spend all your time gorging in Brother Solano's kitchen?"

"Of course not!"

"Then you have seen the men working on the new cathedral?"

Chakoh nodded. "Cowards and weaklings. No true warrior surrenders. It is better to starve."

"Not all those slaves were warriors."

"But they were. Why else would they be slaves?" He pushed away the memory of the frightened Pima telling of the evil hair-faces. Hadn't Cabeza de Vaca said these men were few? And it was common knowledge in the marketplace that the Viceroy had removed the man responsible for the slave raids. That proved the Spaniards were a great and honorable people.

Esteban stared at him a moment. Then he rose and lifted the buckets. "To be sure, you are right to remain in Mexico. You have much to learn."

He strode off without a backward glance. Chakoh rose to follow but thought better of it. When Esteban returned with the empty buckets, he would give him the blue stones and leave. He would wait a few days before coming again to the stable. It would be hard, but perhaps then Esteban would be himself again. He groped inside his breeches for the buckskin bag and removed the turquoise. Esteban had stopped to instruct a slave in repairing a wooden stirrup. Chakoh jiggled the stones impatiently.

A boy dressed in clothes like his own came from the

palace and stood staring around the stableyard. He saw Chakoh, waved, and walked over.

"How goes it?" asked the boy.

"It goes well," said Chakoh.

"Do you know which one of these slaves is called Esteban?"

Chakoh blinked. "There must be a mistake."

"No mistake. The Viceroy himself told me to bring him the slave called Esteban from the stables. I guess that Fray Marcos must want to talk to him."

Esteban didn't know Fray Marcos. There must be another Esteban here. Chakoh sighed with relief. "That's *one* Esteban over there. I don't know the other one."

"Are there two?" The boy looked worried. "I have to get the right one. I'll ask this one if he belongs to Dorantes. I hope he tells me the truth."

There might be two Estebans, but there was only one Dorantes could have owned. No, it couldn't be. Esteban was brave and his word was never broken. Esteban could never be a slave. But suddenly he saw the true meaning of many things Dorantes had said. There could be no doubt. It was true.

Esteban was a slave, no better than the Indians who carried their shame branded on their cheek.

"No," he cried to himself. "That's not true."

But it had to be. How else could a man like Dorantes have captured Esteban?

Again he thought of the slave raiders, but surely that had been only once. Even if it had happened before, certainly Esteban would have fought. Unless Esteban was not what he'd seemed to be.

Chakoh's vision blurred and shimmered. Esteban was a liar. He was none of the things he'd pretended. Chakoh clenched the two stones until his nails cut deep into his palm. He would not weep for a slave. His eyes cleared as Esteban approached.

"I must go, little one. The Viceroy calls."

Chakoh didn't dare unclench his teeth for fear of crying. Silently he held out the turquoise.

"You keep them. For you they are good medicine." He reached out to close Chakoh's fingers over the stones.

Chakoh jerked from his touch. "I don't want them. I don't want anything from you."

"What have I done?"

"You lied to me."

"I have never lied to you, little one."

"You are a slave."

"I never said I was not."

That was true, but it made Chakoh feel even more betrayed. His anger grew until he had no room for any other feeling.

"I should have told you," said Esteban sadly. "I tried once but I couldn't."

"Because you are a coward with no sense of shame."

Even as he shouted the words Chakoh knew himself to be the one who lied now. He threw the blue stones at Esteban's feet and ran blindly toward the gate.

He had no memory of crossing the Plaza or walking the abbey halls, but he must have, for when the throbbing ache in his chest became bearable he was sprawled on his bed under the red velvet curtains. Cautiously he drew his new knowledge to the front of his mind and examined it.

At last he understood the feeling of smothered anger that had always hung between Esteban and Dorantes. Chakoh had thought Dorantes followed Esteban from the village of the Buffalo People out of fear, but it had really been to keep his property from wandering away. When Dorantes had been really afraid in the village of the tea drinkers, he'd been willing to abandon Esteban to save himself. No wonder. Esteban was only a slave.

"A slave," Chakoh muttered. He thumped the bed with his fist. "He lied to me."

No, Esteban had never denied he was a slave. But wasn't deliberately not saying it a form of lying? For how else was one to know? There was never a slave like Esteban.

Slaves were miserable excuses for men, dragging hopelessly through their wretched, shortening days. No slave was wise or courageous. If he was, he wouldn't be captured. On that long journey to Mexico Esteban had led them. More than once he had saved them.

Then how had Esteban become a slave? Could it be the

Spaniards who were not honorable? He touched his right cheek as he thought of the slaves working on the cathedral. Had Esteban's words been a warning that Chakoh might become one of them? No, it couldn't be!

"He is a slave," Chakoh shouted. "His word means nothing."

He must not weaken. He must put all thoughts of Esteban from his mind. That would be hard but he must do it.

He leaped from the bed and pulled the loincloth from the bottom of the chest. He would destroy it, tear it, burn it, just as he'd destroy everything that reminded him of Esteban. He glanced out the window that gave a narrow view of the Plaza. His shoulders sagged.

Could he destroy all Mexico? Without Esteban he would not be here. The city itself was a constant reminder of the slave.

Fingers tapped on the door. Fray Marcos opened it and peered in. "Ah, my son, you are here." He pointed to the cloth in Chakoh's hands. "I see that you have already heard the news and are preparing for the journey."

"What journey?"

"But I thought you knew. We are going to Cíbola."

"With Cortez?"

"You have been listening to gossip, my son. Gossip is a sin."

"Yes, Father."

"Coronado, the new governor of Culiacán, will lead the

army. But first the Viceroy wishes you to help guide our little expedition to Cíbola."

Chakoh gaped in amazement. "The Viceroy wants *me* to guide the army?"

"No, my son. No army will assemble until we return. The Viceroy does not wish to empty the King's treasury chasing mirages. He wants to be certain that Cíbola exists before he sends Coronado."

"But it does exist. Aunt Maria's husband has been there."

"I believe you, my son, but we must see for ourselves. Fray Oronato and myself are to explore the country, report on Cíbola and its inhabitants, and inquire about the country beyond. The Viceroy is depending on us."

"Just the three of us?" Chakoh almost laughed at the mighty expedition to Cíbola . . . two priests and a boy.

"Oh, there will be another guide. The Viceroy has rented the slave that was with you."

"Esteban?"

Fray Marcos nodded. "That is why I want you along. I know I can depend on you. Dorantes has warned the Viceroy that the slave is dangerous, unruly, and apt to desert us in time of need."

"That's not true!" He looked away from the priest's frown. "Forgive me, Father."

"I do, for you are young and have much to learn."

"Yes, Father." Chakoh thought of the long trail and the

many campfires he must share with Esteban. Feeling as he did, how could he bear it? If only he could call back the sun and begin the day once more. No, even if such magic were possible, it would change nothing. No matter how often the sun repeated its journey, Esteban was still a slave. But yesterday Chakoh had not known it.

Did that mean that the difference was only in knowing that Esteban was a slave?

That must be so, thought Chakoh. If I had known back in my village, everything would have been different. I would never have been friends with Esteban. I would never have followed him to Mexico. But still Esteban would have been the same. Only I would not have known him. And if it had not been for the page, everything today would have been the same.

What made the difference in knowing? Could it be Chakoh who had changed, or wasn't Esteban ever Esteban?

It was too confusing. His thoughts whirled like the beaters in a cup of chocolate. Somewhere in the dark foaming depths there was an answer. If only he could find it.

He must find it. He could not bear the journey to Cíbola if he didn't.

NINE ✳ RETURN TO THE RIM

The high walls and fruit trees muffled the noise of the city. The quiet of the abbey garden was broken only by the quick rhythmic rasps of the hoes, the soft voices of the brothers and their occasional laughter. Chakoh had spent many afternoons perched in the fruit trees trying to discover the mystery of growing things. He had never heard the brothers sing growing songs or seen them make medicine with the prayer beads. He'd decided they did such things at night, as Aunt Maria's husband did, so he'd abandoned spying on the brothers. Now he was back in the peach tree but for a different reason. This time he was spying on the slaves working on the cathedral.

He shifted carefully on the narrow limb and stared once more at the men clambering about the growing building. How could these plodding, listless men be compared to Esteban? Yet he was a slave as they were. Perhaps the brand made the difference. Esteban had none on his cheek, but neither did the slaves Chakoh had seen in his own land, yet they had the same hopeless look of the branded slaves.

He shook his head. Every attempt to find an answer only confused him more.

"You are up the wrong tree, lad."

Chakoh looked down into Brother Solano's grinning face.

"If you want yam cakes to take with you," said the cook, "you had better pick a few limes."

"Yes, sir."

When Chakoh carried the small green fruit into the kitchen, Brother Solano picked up his grumbling where he'd left off after the morning meal.

"Carrying you off just when there's a little meat on your bones. Fray Marcos never thinks of his stomach. Be sure you set food before him or he'll never remember to eat. Though only the good Lord knows what those heathens will call food."

Chakoh grinned. Brother Solano was a good cook but

Aunt Maria could teach him a few things about making tortillas. The thought reminded him of the Pima villages he'd seen after the slave raids. Cabeza de Vaca had complained to the Viceroy, and the raids had been stopped. The cruel governor of Culiacán had been removed and Coronado appointed in his place. That much Chakoh had learned from Fray Marcos and the market gossip, but he did not understand why the raids had begun.

"Brother Solano, why do the Spaniards make slaves of the Indians?"

"Because they revolt against the King's command."

That was true of the Aztecs, but Chakoh could not imagine the Pima revolting. Besides, they had not been under the King's command. "Is that the only reason?"

"Some refuse to give up their pagan gods and become Christians."

"But what of the slave raiders?"

"They break the law themselves. Ask Fray Marcos about them. He fought them in Peru. Such things are beyond me. Here, have a tortilla."

Chakoh sighed. Food was always the answer when he questioned Brother Solano. It was different with Esteban.

Esteban. If only Chakoh could forget him, but he was always in his thoughts like a cactus thorn festering deep in the finger. He could not imagine Esteban surrendering. The Aztecs had. Chakoh could see them in the Plaza. They were said to be fierce warriors but Chakoh could not be sure. He hadn't known them. But he did know Esteban and Esteban would fight to the death. He was sure of it. Yet he must have thrown down the spear.

"If only I knew why." He was not aware he'd spoken aloud until Brother Solano answered.

"The only way to find the answer is to ask the question. Have another tortilla. They are cold from this morning but they fill the stomach."

"And one cannot ask questions on an empty stomach." Chakoh tried hard not to smile.

"Ah, you see? You are a lad with sense. Why must you go off to the end of the world?"

"Right now I am going only across the Plaza."

Brother Solano was right in one thing. The only way to find the answer was to ask the question.

He found Esteban stacking the hay that Indians were bringing into the stable, loaded on their backs. Esteban glanced down but continued working. Chakoh shuffled nervously and wondered how one asked a man to explain his cowardice.

"How goes it, Esteban?" he asked at last.

"It goes well." Jab went the fork. Up went the hay.

"We are going to Cíbola." Chakoh's neck swiveled as he followed each forkful of hay.

"So I have heard." *Jab. Swish.*

"Must you do that?" Chakoh shouted.

Esteban rested on the fork. "To be sure. I am Esteban,

the valuable property of Captain Andrés Dorantes and now rented like an old plow horse to the Viceroy. And since a horse needs exercise, my dear Viceroy, Esteban can make himself useful by cleaning the stables."

The last sentence was a bitter mimicry of Dorantes' rasping voice. Chakoh remembered the same voice promising to reward Esteban when they reached Mexico. Instead he was lord of the Viceroy's stables. Chakoh saw the true meaning of the title Esteban had given himself. He lowered himself to the pile of hay and tried to sort the questions and the means of asking them. The straightest path was the best.

"I thought you were a brave warrior."

Esteban stared at him. "We did no fighting on the trail."

"I mean before that. Before you were a slave."

"I was never a soldier."

"Then how were you captured?"

"Esteban scratched his head, then settled himself beside Chakoh in the hay.

"Do you remember your village, little one? The starving children with their swollen stomachs, women digging for dry roots, hunters waiting hours for a rat, a man and a boy grinding fish bones one stormy night? Do you remember?"

Chakoh nodded. For the first time in weeks he saw his village as clearly as if he stood in his father's doorway.

"Imagine such a place surrounded by a city large as

Mexico, a city of great wealth with jeweled minarets gleaming in the sun and temples rich with mosaics. Imagine a family in this poor district. A family with seven children, all starving in the midst of wealth. What is there to do?"

Chakoh shook his head helplessly.

"The eldest is sold to save the others."

"You mean your parents *made* you a slave?"

"It is the custom."

"It is a horrible custom."

"To be sure, but I held no bitterness until now."

Chakoh nodded. "I understand. Dorantes promised to reward you. I heard him. He said when he got back to Mexico he would see you were properly rewarded for saving us from the Buffalo People." Suddenly he realized what Esteban had expected. "You were sure he would give you your freedom."

"Twice he promised, but I know my master. His promises are like rainbows, formed in bad weather and vanishing in a clear sky. But I was sure Cabeza de Vaca would help or the Viceroy himself would give me justice. I shared the hardships with the other three. For ten years we shared. What they have done, I have done also. No more, but no less either."

"But you did do more, Esteban. You saved Dorantes and Castillo many times. Why, Dorantes would still be with the Buffalo People if it weren't for you, or we'd have all been killed by those tea drinkers. And you are the one with the gift of tongues, the one the tribes welcomed as they would their own. You saved us all."

"And now I am lord of the Viceroy's stables."

No wonder Esteban had been angry that first day and had warned Chakoh against promises. It seemed the Spaniards might not be as great and honorable as he'd thought, and Chakoh did not welcome the knowledge. Better to forget it and turn his thoughts to bringing Esteban from his dark mood.

"We will soon be going to Cíbola. Then you'll be out of these stables."

Esteban laughed bitterly. "Just as I was taken out of Spain, then taken out of Hispaniola, then out of Cuba to Florida. Now I am being taken out of Mexico." His eyes narrowed and his next words were so low Chakoh had to lean forward to hear.

"So I walk the world's rim once again like a blind horse chained to a waterwheel. Around and around with never an ending."

"I thought you would be glad to be going to Cíbola."

"To be sure, little one. It is a dream come true." But the words were flat and harsh. Esteban stared straight ahead, lost in his thoughts.

Chakoh rose and brushed absently at his doublet. "We leave tomorrow. Things will be better on the trail. Wait and see. Remember Aunt Maria? Perhaps we can trade for more scarecrows."

His voice trailed off. Esteban wasn't listening. He seemed to have forgotten Chakoh though he did murmur, "Go with God, little one."

Chakoh clamped his teeth hard on his lips. He had almost replied, "God have mercy on you," and he didn't know why. It was as if someone else had tried to speak from inside him. Before he entered the crowded Plaza he spat twice over his left shoulder.

That night Chakoh waited impatiently until sure the brothers were settled for the night. He padded barefooted through the kitchen and into the garden. Behind a sheltering row of beans he knelt and prayed long to the Spanish god. After the prayers he opened the medicine bag, formed the Circle of Life with the dried tea leaves and worked the magic of his private medicine. When the soft chants had faded in the night air, he made the sign of the cross, buried the used leaves beneath the bean stalks, and crept back to his room. He was ready for the journey to Cíbola.

The next morning he knelt in the pre-dawn gloom of the church, shivering in the chill dampness. He was no longer accustomed to running nearly naked. He wore only sandals and the cotton cloth that Esteban had given him in Aunt Maria's village. Beside him hunched the massive dark figure of Esteban himself, the familiar gourd rattle in his hand. The bells around Esteban's legs clinked as he rose. Everything was so much like it had been before. And yet it was so different.

Chakoh followed Esteban into the deserted Plaza. Together they watched the soldiers mount. Coronado was to accompany them as far as Culiacán, where Chakoh had first seen horses and buildings. There the commander would assume his new duties as governor, but all Mexico knew that as soon as he received Fray Marcos' report Coronado would be busy assembling the great expedition to Cíbola.

The soldiers rode off, the hoofs of the horses hollow drumbeats on the bridges and dull thuds on the solid road. The two priests followed, their long gray robes dusting their sandal tops. Chakoh and Esteban fell into step, and behind them came the Indian porters carrying supplies on their backs.

A heavy mist clung to the causeway and beaded Chakoh's hair with moisture. Only a few Indians paddling their vegetables to market paused to watch them leave.

"A fitting start to our journey," muttered Esteban.

"It will be better when the sun rises."

Chakoh heel-hopped a victory dance, partly to raise his friend's spirits and partly to warm himself. He succeeded in neither.

Though the mist soon scattered before a chill breeze, heavy gray clouds hid the sun. Before evening a drizzling rain gathered in rivulets down Chakoh's back. They found shelter in one of the buildings the Aztecs had built along the highways for their merchants and tax collectors. All shared the Spanish food that the porters carried for the soldiers.

Chakoh sipped rain water and sighed. "What one needs on a night like this is chocolate sweetened with vanilla."

"You are soft," said Esteban.

"I am not." But he stopped rubbing his aching legs.

"You are a fat grain-fed duckling preening his feathers on the lake of Mexico."

"And what's wrong with that?"

"Nothing, little one, but beware. Food is always used to bait traps."

Chakoh tried to dampen his quick flare of anger. Esteban had no right to criticize all Spaniards because of his bitterness toward Dorantes, but Chakoh had no wish to quarrel either. He answered lightly.

"At least if I am trapped in the abbey, Brother Solano won't let me starve."

Esteban shook his head sadly. "There are worse things than starving."

There was no answer Chakoh could give the brooding slave. He curled up, feet to the fire, and hoped that Esteban would be his old self in the morning.

But he wasn't. Not that morning or any other.

The sun glinted on Coronado's gold helmet, but Esteban's face was dark and gloomy as the day before. Even the bells at his knees had lost their gay jingle and gave forth only an occasional dull clank. Nor did Esteban dance in time to the beat of the gourd rattle. The precious gift from the Buffalo People hung from his loincloth thong. In the evening he held it in his hands, studying it as if it were some strange object he'd just discovered.

It is just the presence of the soldiers, thought Chakoh. Once Coronado was left behind at Culiacán, Esteban would sing again and tell stories the way he'd done before. Patiently Chakoh trudged and waited.

After leaving Culiacán, Chakoh and Esteban took the lead. At midday Esteban trotted ahead to the next village to arrange food and shelter for the night. Chakoh followed more slowly with the priests. As they approached the village the Indians came out to welcome the priests with the sign of the cross taught them by the three Señors. Sleeping places were ready for their use. The best food was set before them. Fray Marcos was delighted but Chakoh could only stare in disbelief.

What had happened to the villages since he'd been here? They were much smaller than he'd remembered. The great fields were only poor patches of stunted corn, not anything like the ones he'd seen near Mexico. Even the food disappointed him. The cornmeal was coarse and gritty, the stews flavorless without salt and spices. Most of all Chakoh missed meat.

The cotton cloth that had once delighted him no longer seemed a miracle. He couldn't help comparing the plain narrow strips with the colorful clothes he'd left in Mexico. The woven sleeping mats scratched and certainly the ground beneath them had hardened since last he slept upon it. The chill drafts could not be closed out or the huts would fill with eye-burning smoke. It was a terrible way to live.

It was the way he'd lived most of his life! The way his parents still lived, except they had no cloth or food. To them a Pima village would be as marvelous as the heaven the priests spoke about. His throat tightened as he remembered his mother's tears that last day and the medicine shell his father had placed around his neck. Then he remembered the winter and the hunger.

Most likely his parents were thankful they had one less mouth to feed. And if he could not find comfort in a Pima village, how could Chakoh bear the home of his father?

The next morning Chakoh set a pace that stretched even Esteban's legs to their limit.

"What is the hurry, little one?"

"The sooner we get to Cíbola, the sooner I will be back in Mexico."

"You are thinking of Brother Solano's kitchen."

"It is all the same." He was sorry they'd eaten the yam cakes so quickly. As long as they'd lasted, Mexico had seemed very near. His own land had faded again from his memory. Perhaps Mexico's wonders would vanish also and he would be content to eat what Brother Solano called heathen food. Chakoh shuddered and pushed forward. Once he returned to Mexico, not even the Viceroy would persuade him to leave it again.

They soon reached the river where Chakoh and Esteban had sailed the boats. They laughed about it over the evening cookfire.

"Those were good times," sighed Chakoh.

"With a head so full of new useful things you learned in Mexico, I am surprised that you remember the boats."

"I remember many things." It was becoming more difficult to smother his anger.

"Do you remember how it was to climb the mountain passes, the wind in your face and the new land spread out at your feet? Do you remember waking each morning with the day like an empty jar to fill as you pleased?"

"I remember fingers bleeding from digging lizards from frozen ground. My bones remember cold, and my stomach remembers the cramp of hunger. That is what I remember and what I wish to forget."

"You are a fool," snapped Esteban. Then he grinned. "But you are a young fool, so there is hope."

Chakoh's only answer was to move away and curl up by himself. During the night he woke shivering and decided to forgive Esteban. He groped his way to the ash-coated embers and took his accustomed place against Esteban's broad back. In a few moments he was warm enough to sleep.

He roused once during the night to find nothing behind him but the warm place where Esteban had lain. The gourd rattle bulged reassuringly against his thigh. Esteban would return. He yawned and hugged himself into a ball against the chill. When he woke at dawn the rattle was gone and Esteban was nowhere in the village.

TEN ✱ QUARRELS

The Gray Robe was sick, said the villagers. Not the Gray Robe that was thin as a cornstalk but the other one. All night he had been sick. The Dark One had left before dawn with two of the men from the village. No one knew when they would return. Some said the Dark One was not coming back.

Where had Esteban gone? And why? Chakoh squinted at the pale horizon as if he could find the answer there.

Fray Marcos called. Chakoh ducked into the hut. Fray Oronato lay on the sleeping mat. His breath came in shallow gasps. Sweat rolled down his face, and his hands twitched on his chest.

"He has been like this most of the night," said Fray Marcos.

"Have you made medicine?" whispered Chakoh.

"I have done all I can, but he will not be able to travel for a while. I am sure he will recover, but the delay is serious. That is why I have sent Esteban ahead."

"You *sent* him." The words came softly in a breath of relief. Chakoh had carried the fear that Esteban had run away.

The worry lines deepened in the priest's thin face. "I pray I have not made a mistake. So much depends on our success."

He explained the system they'd devised to send messages. As soon as Esteban found news of the trail to Cíbola he would send back one of the villagers with a cross. The size of the cross would indicate the greatness of the news. A small cross would mean he was still searching. One large as his hand would mean good news.

"He suggested it," the priest finished. "It seemed the best thing to do, but now I wonder. Dorantes warned he was unreliable."

"Esteban will not fail you."

But he was not so sure of that two days later when a pair

of Indians staggered into the village carrying a cross larger than a man.

Fray Marcos was overjoyed. "He must be at the edge of Cíbola itself or very close to it."

Chakoh tried to tell him that Esteban could not yet have reached Aunt Maria's village and Cíbola was far beyond that. Fray Marcos was too excited to listen.

"Fray Oronato will be himself in a week or so, but we cannot wait so long, not with such good news. I shall arrange for him to be guided back to Culiacán." He sent the Indian messengers back to Esteban with instructions to wait where he was. "Tell him we follow at once."

But Esteban did not wait. At each village the Gray Robe was expected. The Dark One had asked them to prepare food and lodgings for the Gray Robe who followed, but Esteban himself was always just beyond the next village, the next river, the next mountain. The farther they went, the more furious Fray Marcos grew at this disobedience to orders. Twice he had sent other Indians to Esteban with instructions to wait.

"If you go on alone, do you think you can catch that slave?" he asked Chakoh.

"I will try." Though he'd grown since last he'd traveled this trail, Esteban's legs were still longer and his strength greater.

"Then go. And wherever you find him, tell him I order him to remain there until I come."

"Yes, Father." He hesitated. Fray Marcos continually stopped to question the Indians about the country to the east and west. Chakoh translated both questions and answers. "Who will interpret for you?"

"I will do my best with signs. Go now, my son."

Without the priest to slow him Chakoh covered ground twice as quickly. Late the second afternoon he caught up with Esteban and more than forty Indians who had joined him along the way.

Esteban shook the rattle in greeting. "How goes it, little one? And where is the good father?"

"At *his* pace, at least three days back. Perhaps four."

"So far? Then we shall camp early tonight."

"Choose a good place with plenty of water. Fray Marcos orders you to wait until he comes."

Esteban closed his eyes and breathed deeply as if testing the northern breeze. "I have far to go, little one."

"But you will wait?"

"No."

Chakoh's chin dropped and his feet took root. Esteban moved on. The Indians crowded past, laughing and singing. Chakoh followed slowly. He made no effort to catch up with Esteban. There would be time for argument when camp was made. Until then he must accustom himself to this man who behaved as Esteban should but spoke like a stranger.

They halted at the edge of a steep-banked stream. With

his ready laugh and a few bantering words Esteban had even the idlers hurrying for firewood and filling water gourds. Before the sun touched the mountain ridge they were sharing corn cakes and roast rabbit. The Pima gathered at separate fires to sing, talk, or play the bean game. Everything was so much the way it had been before that Chakoh half expected to see the three Señors at their evening prayers.

He sprawled beside Esteban and sighed contentedly. "It goes well, Esteban."

"To be sure." He squinted along the stick he was carving and nodded in approval.

"I don't mean that," said Chakoh. "I mean the journey to Cíbola."

Esteban nodded gravely. "Yes, that too goes well. Even better than I had expected."

"Then why must you spoil it?"

Esteban's hands were still. "What I do will not change the father's plans."

"Then you will wait here for him?"

"No." He placed the finished carving on the ground and selected another stick from a bundle at his side. They looked like arrow shafts except that Esteban was carving three waving lines down their length. Something tugged at Chakoh's memory.

"You must wait." Chakoh frowned at the carved stick. "I told Fray Marcos you would not fail him."

"And I will not. I said that I would find the trail to Cíbola and prepare the Indians for his arrival. I shall keep my promise."

"But you will not obey his order."

Esteban looked up in mock surprise. "Has Fray Marcos arrived already? If not, how can he give me an order? I hear only your words. How do I know they come from my master?"

"So that is why you were so eager to come on alone."

"And the reason I stay well beyond the range of the father's voice."

"The gods smile on you," said Chakoh bitterly. "How fortunate that Fray Oronato became ill."

"Yes, for I would not have liked giving him a drink of your tea, little one."

"Esteban, you never would have done such a thing!"

Esteban shrugged. Chakoh stared down at his crossed legs.

"Why should I doubt it? It is no more dishonorable than refusing to obey your master's orders."

"I am not refusing. I have been passed from master to master. First Dorantes, then the Viceroy, and now Fray Marcos. I have served each well. If Fray Marcos speaks, I shall obey. But unless I hear the words directly from the father's lips, how can I be sure the orders come from him? I cannot heed every man and boy who meets me on the trail. So I follow my master's last orders; scout the trail to

Cíbola and send back word of my discoveries."

Esteban's private rules bound him to his master's commands, but only if he heard them from Fray Marcos himself. It was the same as when he had said nothing of being a slave. Chakoh could not say it was wrong but he felt it was not entirely right. He picked up the carved stick Esteban had just finished.

"Your honor is like the line you carved on this shaft. It carefully avoids the knobs and knots." But there were no irregularities on the shaft. It was straight and true, unmarred except for the useless carved grooves. Once before he'd seen arrow shafts carved like these.

"It *is* an arrow shaft." Chakoh gripped it in both hands and stared at Esteban. "The arrow of the buffalo hunters."

"To be sure."

In two days Esteban would reach Aunt Maria's village. He need only travel northeast until he reached the river, then follow it to the mountains and beyond to the land of the Buffalo People.

"You're deserting. You're running away just as Dorantes said you would."

Esteban put down his work and gazed thoughtfully at Chakoh. "You think that is wrong, little one?"

"I *know* it is wrong. You have been sent on a mission and now you abandon it."

"To be sure," Esteban said softly. "And what of your mission, little one?"

Chakoh could easily guide Fray Marcos to Aunt Maria's village, but what then? It was Esteban who had won the friendship of the Indians, Esteban they followed even now. Esteban would have no trouble persuading Aunt Maria's husband to guide Fray Marcos to Cíbola, but Chakoh was sure the Pima would risk the journey for no one else.

"My mission will fail," he said bitterly. "We can never reach Cíbola without you."

The shaft in Esteban's hand snapped. He tossed it into the fire. "It is no use. Your mind follows only one trail."

"At least it follows the trail on which it was sent."

"Does it still follow the trail on which your father sent you?"

Chakoh was too surprised to answer. What had this to do with Cíbola or Esteban's desertion?

"Why did your father send you to Mexico?"

"To learn of the Spanish god."

"Why?"

"So my people could overcome the Spirit-of-Misfortune." He tried to ignore the uneasy stirring of guilt. "I still follow that trail."

"You follow your stomach. Dangle Brother Solano's kitchen before your nose and you sit slavering like a dog at a meat-drying rack. And like the dog, you remain only because of the promise of food."

The fear that Esteban was right only heightened the anger his guilt had raised in self-defense.

"That's not true," he shouted. "I still have many things to learn."

"To be sure. You have not yet learned the manners of a *don*. You have not yet learned to fawn and flatter those in power or to barter for a favor. You cannot yet smile while you lie or turn traitor to your friends."

Chakoh jumped to his feet. "I will hear no more."

"So you have learned one thing. To turn your back on the truth."

"It is not the truth. You're only bitter because of the way Dorantes treated you. As for betraying friends, what are you doing now?"

He shouted down Esteban's attempt to interrupt. "The Viceroy will be furious if we fail to reach Cíbola. All of Mexico is waiting for the expedition to begin. Fray Marcos said the future of Spain depends on our success. Now we will fail because you care only for your freedom."

Esteban's face wore the look of a man in mourning, but his laugh was bitter and harsh. "I did not know you cared so deeply for the future of Spain. What is my freedom compared to that?"

"Then you will wait here and guide Fray Marcos to Cíbola?"

"I will lead Fray Marcos to Cíbola."

"A thousand thanks, Esteban."

The dark head shook sadly. "Do not thank me. I hoped you would come with me to the Buffalo People. From there you could easily return home."

"Surely you didn't think I'd leave Mexico?"

"It is better to be a warrior in a mat hut than a beggar in the Plaza."

"I would rather be a beggar than a . . ." His tongue still curled on the word *slave,* but from the look on Esteban's face he might just as well have said it. He wished the Night Demons would snatch him away to be tossed forever on the north wind. Anything would be better than to stand here with the cold silence stretching between them.

"There is a moon tonight," he said at last. "Fray Marcos will be eager to hear that you are waiting. I shall start back."

Not until he was beyond sight of the campfires did Chakoh realize that Esteban had not answered. He had not even said, "Go with God." Perhaps the Night Demons would get him. Fear kept him awake and moving all night. Whenever he stopped to rest, the sigh of the wind or the shadow over the moon would start his heart pounding and he'd move on. He knew he could not escape if the Night Demons found him, but moving eased the fear.

He plodded on after sunrise until he found a spring. He drank lightly and leaned against a rock until his body cooled and he could drink again. When he woke it was late afternoon. Fray Marcos and two grinning Pima stood over him. Every traveler stopped at water. If he had slept anywhere else he would have missed them.

Assured that Esteban would wait, Fray Marcos once more stopped in the villages to ask questions. Chakoh was glad of the delay. He could not forget Esteban's face when the unspoken word *slave* had hung between them. Not even Esteban could forgive him that.

As they neared Esteban's camp Chakoh lagged in the rear, ashamed to face Esteban. He need not have worried. Nothing remained on the river bank but the black circles of the campfires.

"But he promised to wait," said Chakoh. "Why would he leave?"

"Because he has run away." The priest's voice was bitter. "What else could I expect of a slave?"

Chakoh stared at him. Of course a slave would run away. Hadn't he himself told Esteban that a slave with any sense of honor should try to escape even if it meant death from his captors? How then could he blame Esteban for fleeing to the Buffalo People?

His thoughts were interrupted by the sight of two Indians coming toward them on the trail. Between them they bore another huge cross. And again Chakoh wondered why.

He knew Esteban had heard nothing new of Cíbola. Aunt Maria had already told them all anyone in her village knew, and one of the messengers was from that village. Why send the over-sized cross that meant great news? Surely Esteban knew it would bring Fray Marcos on the run. Why keep the priest on the trail if he was deserting?

At sight of the second large cross Fray Marcos tucked his

robes around his waist and set a pace that would have awed an antelope. Chakoh trotted ahead scouting and worrying.

Did the cross mean that Esteban would wait at Aunt Maria's? For Esteban had promised to wait. No, he had not said he would wait. He had said he would lead Fray Marcos to Cíbola. Was that another curve on Esteban's shaft of honor? Did he mean he would keep just ahead of them on the trail to Cíbola?

The thought should have made him happy, but the feelings it roused were too strange and confused for Chakoh to understand. He almost hoped Esteban was far up the river to the Buffalo People, stealing the freedom Dorantes had promised and refused.

Another part of him feared what Mexico would be like if Esteban had deserted and their mission failed. Would the Viceroy have him branded on the cheek and sent to work on the cathedral? Surely Fray Marcos would not permit that. But the three Señors had returned in triumph from an impossible journey and look what had happened to them. And to Esteban.

Esteban was a slave, Chakoh told himself.

Another voice inside him whispered, and you are only an Indian like the Aztecs.

With each step his feelings changed from hope that Esteban was leading them to Cíbola to fear that he was not. And mixed with both was the thought that Esteban deserved his freedom.

"But not this way," he whispered to himself. "Not after he promised. Not Esteban." But he wasn't sure.

Fray Marcos had taken no time from the trail that day for food. Chakoh's stomach rumbled and he thought longingly of Brother Solano's heaping platters of food, but he did not remind Fray Marcos to eat. He was too eager to reach the village. Even if Esteban was not waiting, Aunt Maria would know which trail he had taken.

ELEVEN ✳ THE DESERTER

"Ah, Chakoh! I thought never to see you again. Those strangers from the north—"

"From Cíbola?" interrupted Chakoh.

Aunt Maria nodded. "The same. They returned this way soon after you left. They made angry talk about hair-faces who made slaves of the people."

"The three Señors who were with me last time have stopped that. There is nothing to fear now."

The old woman nodded. "They were good men. We saw

that. But all the same I feared for you. I thought you would be made a slave and we should never have you sitting beneath our roof again. Then the Dark One came and said it was true."

An angry reply rose to Chakoh's lips but the twinkle in Aunt Maria's eyes stopped it.

"And what did the Dark One say?" he asked instead.

"He said that you were a slave to your stomach." She clucked and shook her head. "But you are so worn and thin, I cannot believe it. Come, you must eat."

"Ask about Esteban," ordered Fray Marcos.

Chakoh obeyed.

"He has gone ahead," said Aunt Maria.

Fray Marcos was furious, but Chakoh's surge of joy almost drowned his dread of facing Esteban. Surely this meant Esteban was leading the father to Cíbola as he'd promised.

"Now not another word until you've eaten." But Aunt Maria's words did not apply to herself. As Chakoh and the priest ate she worked at a new basket and kept up a steady stream of chatter, all of it about Esteban.

"The charms he made to guard our fields were falling down. Some had lost their heads or were blind. Though he was in a great hurry, he took time to restore them for us."

Chakoh stared out at the fields, each with one of Esteban's ragged scarecrows. That had been a good time. He remembered others. He remembered laughing as Esteban played the Man-Chased-by-Buffalo, racing boats on a flooded river, even hunting lizards had been an adventure with Esteban. He could remember no time with Esteban that had not been good until Mexico. What had happened to him?

Aunt Maria pressed another cactus fruit into his hand, but Chakoh chewed it without knowing what he ate.

"You were like brothers," the woman said.

Chakoh nodded. "We walked the rim of the world together."

Now Esteban walked it alone. Perhaps he would have been able to stop if he'd gone to the Buffalo People. Or would they have forgotten Man-Chased-by-Buffalo? Perhaps, like the Circle of Life, Esteban would go round and round with never an end. Hadn't he said it himself?

Aunt Maria prodded his sandal. "Did you hear me?"

"You said we were like brothers."

She looked hurt. "That was a long time ago."

"I am sorry."

"You should be. It was all about you. The Dark One said you wish to make your home in the land of the hairfaces."

"That is true."

She clucked disapprovingly. "How can you let your brother walk the long trail alone."

"But the Gray Robe and I follow."

"The Dark One said you wish to travel to Cíbola so that you can return to the hair-faces as a great warrior and live among them in honor."

"That is true."

"Then you do not follow your brother."

She said more, but Chakoh heard nothing but the thoughts pounding in his own head. Esteban had lied. He had broken his promise. He said he would lead them but he lied.

Chakoh jerked his head to clear it. After all, Esteban was only a slave. What honor had a slave? Yet with all his doubts Chakoh would sooner have expected the sun to travel south to north than for Esteban to break his word. Slave or free, Esteban was still Esteban. Chakoh held his breath so the thought would not escape.

What had really hurt him that day in the stableyard? Was it the knowledge that Esteban was a slave or the fear that he had lied? If it was because Esteban was a slave, was that only because Chakoh had thought all slaves were cowards with no honor? For that would mean Esteban was not worthy of the love and friendship Chakoh had given. Then he had heard Esteban's story of being sold into slavery and he'd known the man was no coward defeated in battle. Once more he had placed his trust in Esteban but not as fully as before. Anger and suspicion had remained.

Why? Because he could no longer hold fast to what he'd been taught about slaves? For no longer could he believe that all slaves were cowards with no sense of honor. Esteban proved it was false. His courage was even greater than Dorantes'. As for honor, what had Esteban said? A slave can find honor in serving his master. Because he had gone willingly into slavery to save his family, Esteban had served his master well.

Chakoh squirmed uneasily. He saw now the reason he could not admit he'd been wrong about slaves. For if that was false it meant that Esteban was right about the Spanish God and the Spirit-of-Misfortune being one and the same. It meant Esteban was right about other things, things too painful for Chakoh to think of.

I am not a slave to my stomach, thought Chakoh angrily. I have not deserted my mission. I wish to remain in Mexico only because the Spanish have much to teach me.

But suppose Esteban was right? No, he couldn't be. Chakoh groped desperately for an excuse not to admit it even to himself. He found one.

Hadn't Aunt Maria just said they walked different trails? That could only mean that Esteban now traveled northeast along the river to the land of the buffalo hunters. Esteban had broken his word. And the thought soothed his own feelings of guilt.

Aunt Maria said softly, "The Dark One wished to say farewell to his brother."

"Then why did he not wait?"

"He said you no longer wished to share his campfire."

Chakoh hung his head as he remembered their last quarrel. He had learned much since then. If only he could let Esteban know. But Esteban was gone. And there had been no one to wish him to go with God.

"If only I could have seen him once more."

"Then follow him," said Aunt Maria.

"I cannot. I must go to Cíbola."

"Cíbola is made of stone. It will always be there. But what of the Dark One?"

Mexico had been lonely enough this past winter, but at least he'd had the faint hope of finding Esteban. He remembered what it had been like when he'd decided Esteban was dead, when he'd thought never again to see that dark head tilt back to let the laughter roll free. Now it was even worse, for Esteban was gone with the memory of their last quarrel hanging between them. Never could Chakoh erase it. Never could he let Esteban know how wrong he'd been.

Chakoh gazed to the northeast. What if Esteban wasn't guiding them to Cíbola as he'd promised? The slave wanted nothing but his freedom, just as Chakoh wanted nothing but to return to Mexico. It was the only chance Esteban would have, just as going to Cíbola was Chakoh's only hope of a good life in Mexico. How then could he blame Esteban?

In the long silence Fray Marcos again complained of Esteban's disobedience to his orders to wait.

"I know you relayed my message, my son. But since Esteban has chosen to disobey, how shall we find the trail to Cíbola? You do not know the country beyond."

"Aunt Maria, I know that your husband is no longer young, but would he guide the Gray Robe to Cíbola?"

"My husband is with the Dark One."

Chakoh's first feeling was one of joy. Esteban wanted so much to see him that he'd taken Aunt Maria's husband with him, knowing Chakoh would have to follow. There was no way they could reach Cíbola unless he brought Aunt Maria's husband back. Esteban would be camped a few days beyond, waiting for him. Then doubt and anger swept over him.

Esteban could be using Aunt Maria's husband as he'd used the huge crosses with Fray Marcos. This could be a lure to get Chakoh to follow, never quite catching up, until he'd drawn the boy all the way to the Buffalo People. Then there'd be nothing for Chakoh to do but return home. Esteban had never wanted Chakoh to remain in Mexico.

"But only because he cared for me," Chakoh whispered.

Chakoh had planned to send Fray Marcos with Aunt Maria's husband while he trailed Esteban and shared one last campfire with his friend. He had wanted them to part with memories they could smile upon. Now he would trail Esteban for another reason. He must bring Aunt Maria's husband back to guide them.

He rose and glanced at the sun. "I must go now and find the Dark One quickly."

Aunt Maria pushed herself to her feet. "I will call my brothers to guide you."

"I can find the way." He could find his way to the river.

From there it was a long but easy trail to the buffalo country.

"You will need someone to help carry water. It is a long dry trail."

Chakoh nodded. Perhaps the river was dry at this season. He would trust Aunt Maria to know best. He turned to Fray Marcos.

"I am going after Esteban."

"Tell him that he must wait for me. Is there someone here who can guide me to the next village or two?"

"You will have to wait here until I return."

"No, we have wasted too much time already."

He dared not tell Fray Marcos that Esteban was no longer on the trail to Cíbola. Not until Esteban was safe in the land beyond the mountains. In desperation he turned to Aunt Maria.

"Is there no one else in the village who knows the trail to Cíbola?"

She laughed. "So many have used it recently that even a small child could follow it. I will send the Gray Robe on tomorrow. Do not worry. You will meet him later. Now hurry. Remember that my home will be empty until you return."

"Go with God." Fray Marcos blessed him.

Though bewildered, Chakoh had no choice but to follow Aunt Maria's two brothers out of the village. They traveled like warriors, resting only briefly during the night and eating on the walk. The water gourds were used sparingly. Chakoh could not understand how the men could travel on so little water. He dreaded the thought of what the hot afternoon would be like.

Tired, hungry, and dry of mouth Chakoh trotted with head bent, following the pair of sandals ahead of him. The day was more than half gone before he realized his shadow was so far to his right that he had to turn his head to see it. He raised his head and squinted at the mountains. They should be traveling a little to the east but they weren't. They were going directly north.

He forced himself ahead to ask the Pima, "Where are we going?"

"To meet the Dark One." The man stared at him so strangely that Chakoh dropped back in line and asked no more questions.

The next day they reached water and a village. The dry time was over, but it brought little relief to Chakoh. Though they passed many villages, they did not stop. Then, on the third day, they saw Esteban's dust in the valley ahead. At every village men had joined Esteban. Nearly a hundred now followed his prancing feet and swishing gourd rattle.

"The Dark One has strong medicine," said one of Chakoh's guides.

"Let us hurry." Chakoh wondered if Esteban planned to take these Pima all the way to the Buffalo People. And why had he not taken the trail they'd traveled before? By tonight he'd know the answers to all his questions. According to his guides they would overtake Esteban at the next village soon after dark.

Chakoh spent the time planning what he would say. He would walk right up and say, "I have come for Aunt Maria's husband."

No, that would not do. It sounded like a Spanish soldier. Better to say, "I understand why you have deserted us and I hold no anger."

Chakoh shook his head. That sounded like Fray Marcos. Perhaps he should apologize for that last time and then demand Aunt Maria's husband. He practiced other phrases, but when he finally walked up to the cookfire and looked across at his friend's face, all he said was, "How goes it, Esteban?"

The familiar grin creased the dark face. "It goes well, little one. Have some venison."

Chakoh dropped to the ground and accepted the food eagerly. It was as if the months in Mexico and since had never been. Then Aunt Maria's husband walked through the edge of the firelight and Chakoh remembered why he was here.

"Esteban, I know you are going to the Buffalo People."

The dark head nodded.

"I have not told Fray Marcos. I was afraid he would follow and order you to return." Though now that Este-

✳ 150

ban had broken his word, Chakoh didn't know if an order from his master would have any effect on the slave's desertion.

"A thousand thanks, little one."

"But I must have Aunt Maria's husband to guide us to Cíbola."

Chakoh fidgeted through the long silence that followed. Was Esteban going to refuse? Would he carry Chakoh off to the Buffalo People?

"Esteban," he said at last. "I *must* guide Fray Marcos to Cíbola. If I don't, I cannot return to Mexico."

"And what will you do in Mexico, little one?"

Chakoh stared at him, hoping there would not be another quarrel.

"Can you bear arms in the service of the King?" asked Esteban. "Or do you have a trade to serve those who do bear arms? You must have something the Spaniards want, to be welcome."

"You are throwing my words back at me." He groped for a way to strike back. "Perhaps the gift of laughter will no longer be enough for the Buffalo People to welcome you."

"It will be enough until I learn their ways."

"I can learn a trade or something."

"To be sure, little one, but you learn slowly. I would not want you to be a beggar in the Plaza."

Chakoh winced at the memory those words brought.

Then he lifted his head proudly and looked unwaveringly into Esteban's eyes. It needed all his courage, but he would say it.

"A beggar lives on the hunting of others, like a buzzard or a maggot. I would rather be a slave than a beggar. At least a slave can keep his honor."

Esteban smiled. His eyes blinked rapidly.

"To be sure, little one." Then he laughed and sent Chakoh sprawling with a playful blow on the back. "There is hope for you yet. Here, little one. Keep these for a time of great need."

Once again the two blue stones lay in Chakoh's hand. They would mean great wealth for Esteban in the buffalo country yet he'd given them to Chakoh.

"I can think of no need great enough for me to part with them. A thousand thanks, Esteban."

Esteban rubbed his nose briskly with the back of his hand and coughed. "Now rest, little one. We leave before dawn."

"But I am going to Cíbola."

"To be sure. We are all going to Cíbola."

"But you said you were returning to the Buffalo People."

"I also said I would lead Fray Marcos to Cíbola. Surely you did not think I would break my promise?"

Chakoh hung his head.

"I want only to stay far enough ahead of Fray Marcos

that his voice cannot reach me. He will find a welcome in every village. I shall tell the people of Cíbola that he is a great medicine man and comes in peace. When I am sure he will be welcomed there, I shall go east to the buffalo country."

"But if Aunt Maria's husband stays with you, who will guide Fray Marcos?"

Esteban waved his hand at the many followers about the fires. "An expedition such as this leaves a well-marked trail, even beyond the villages."

Aunt Maria had said that even a child could follow. She'd known where Esteban was going. Why hadn't she told him? He thought back over the words. She had never said Esteban was not going to Cíbola. Truly, what people did not say was more important than what they spoke. It was clear from what Aunt Maria did say that Esteban wished to see him.

If I had known he was going to Cíbola, thought Chakoh, I wonder if I would have come? Probably not. Shameful memories would have kept him lagging in the rear, convinced there was plenty of time to make amends at Cíbola. It needed the shock of Aunt Maria's words to bring him to this campfire.

Chakoh grinned. Esteban had not been sure words would be enough. He had let Chakoh believe he was taking Aunt Maria's husband to the Buffalo Country. Chakoh could imagine the two of them plotting, planning what to say and what to leave unsaid. They had not known that Chakoh had already discovered that Esteban was still Esteban even if he did bend his honor to suit himself.

But perhaps everyone did. Hadn't Dorantes and Cabeza de Vaca forgotten Esteban when it suited them to? Perhaps Chakoh was doing it himself when he denied it was Brother Solano's kitchen that drew him back to Mexico. Certainly he had bent his honor when he'd told Fray Marcos only half the reason he was going to find Esteban. One could not live without bending one's honor at some time. But like a bent bow, honor would spring back. The important thing was not to break it, as Dorantes had done.

He yawned and wondered if Fray Marcos ever bent his honor. Chakoh doubted it. Perhaps that was what made Fray Marcos a priest. The thought reminded him to warn Esteban.

"Fray Marcos is not far behind. He is very angry that you have not waited for him."

"I will send him another cross tomorrow. That will keep him in good humor."

"That will only make him angrier."

"Then I shall not send it." Esteban stretched out with his feet to the dying fire. Chakoh lay down beside him.

"Tell me how you came to my country."

"Not now, little one."

"It has been a long time, Esteban."

With a soft chuckle Esteban began to tell of the ships

leaving Cuba. Chakoh forced himself to stay awake to the end.

"Tomorrow night will you do the Man-Chased-by-Buffalo?"

"To be sure."

"Strange, is it not? Most of all I wanted to see a great ship and a bullfight in Mexico. I have seen neither."

"You are not likely to see the ship there, little one."

"Nor a bullfight either," thought Chakoh. For he could not bear to go without Esteban.

The next night they had no time for things of the past. At sunset they stood on a hillside and stared across the desert at a red mesa. Atop it rose the walls of Cíbola, pink in the setting sun.

Tomorrow they would enter the city of gold, turquoise, and emeralds. Chakoh could think of nothing but the future. And from the way that Esteban's eyes stared toward the buffalo country, neither could he.

TWELVE ✳ CÍBOLA

Esteban was like a warrior at his first Victory Dance. He tied the bells more securely around his legs, arranged feathers in his hair and flicked dust from those decorating his rattle.

"And now the lord of the Viceroy's stables is prepared to meet the headman of Cíbola," he announced.

There was no need to send a messenger ahead. The men of the pueblo had discovered their presence and were waiting at the foot of the mesa. Truly they were strange people. Their hair was cut off at the level of their chins. Necklaces of the blue stones lay heavy on their chests. Chakoh might have laughed at their short skirts if they hadn't handled their bows and spears in the manner of men expert in their use.

Esteban signaled his followers to wait and stepped forward with only Aunt Maria's husband, who knew enough of the language to interpret. Esteban spoke long and earnestly. From his gestures Chakoh knew he was telling of Fray Marcos and the Spaniards to the south. Then he held out the gourd rattle. With a slap of the hand the headman of Cíbola knocked it to the ground. Aunt Maria's husband retrieved it and handed it to Esteban.

There was more talk, this time from the Cíbolan.

Esteban replied.

The headman gestured. The Cíbolans swarmed over Esteban. They carried him up the mesa trail, up the ladder, and over the wall. When the last Cíbolan was inside the city, the ladder followed. It happened so quickly that Aunt Maria's husband was still standing bewildered, his hands outstretched, when Chakoh rushed up.

"What are they doing with Esteban?"

"They are holding him prisoner."

"I can see that," snapped Chakoh. "But what will they do with him?"

"They will hold council to decide."

"We will rescue him."

By now the Pima were crowding around them. They shook their heads at the suggestion of rescue. It was impossible. Once the ladders were pulled up no one could get into the pueblo. With arrows and rocks the Cíbolans could fight off any war party.

Chakoh stared up at the tiers of walls, one atop the other like a man-made cliff. Somewhere in that city Esteban was a prisoner, and there was nothing Chakoh could do but wait. He paced back and forth along the mesa.

"Why?" he asked. "What did Esteban say to make them angry?"

"He said he came from the white men to the south," replied Aunt Maria's husband.

"There is nothing wrong with that."

"No, but it is strange that white men should send a black man as messenger. Then they began to understand that the white men were the same hair-faces their traders met."

Chakoh nodded. "Your wife told me they had passed through your village and spoken angrily of the slave raiders."

"They believe the hair-faces will come and try to make them slaves. Esteban told them they would not. He told them the Gray Robe is a man of peace, a good man. I assured them that neither the Gray Robe nor the Dark One would harm them."

"That is true."

"But it does not matter. They believe the hair-faces are coming only for slaves. They say they should kill the black one and any others that are sent, as a warning. Then the hair-faces will stay in their own country."

Chakoh stared up at the wall. Aunt Maria's husband patted his arm.

"Do not worry. They will not kill him until the council is over and they may decide to set him free. They are strange people. One can never tell what they will do."

All day and all night Esteban lay in the small window-less room of the pueblo without food or water. At the foot of the mesa his friends waited.

In the hours before dawn Chakoh opened his medicine bag and carefully drew the Circle of Life. Then he closed his eyes and repeated the prayers the priests in Mexico had taught him.

When the first rays of the sun lit the walls of the pueblo, a ladder was pushed over. One by one the Cíbolans came down to the mesa. Then a tall dark figure appeared on the wall.

"They are releasing Esteban," cried Chakoh. He hurried forward to greet his friend.

Esteban climbed down the ladder and walked to the foot of the mesa. As he passed through the ring of Cíbolans one of them pushed him and shouted. Esteban began to run.

Bows lifted. Arrows whined.

Esteban stumbled, recovered, and staggered on. Then like a tree struck by lightning, the great body swayed, toppled, and thudded to the ground.

"Esteban!" Heedless of the arrows Chakoh raced toward his friend. "Esteban!"

He knelt and rolled the heavy body on its back. Desperately he rubbed one hand between his own, calling Esteban over and over. But the hands, so large but so gentle, would never again fashion boats or scarecrows. The dark face tilted back toward the sky, but no laughter poured forth. The eyes mirrored nothing, no joy, no mischief, not even sorrow. Esteban would walk the rim of the world no longer.

Near his outstretched hand lay the gourd rattle, gift of the Buffalo People for the joy he had given. Chakoh reached out and picked it up. He knelt there staring down at the gourd trimmed with red and white feathers.

Rocking back and forth in his grief he cried aloud, "Why didn't you go to them? Why didn't you leave us and go when you could?"

But even as he spoke he knew Esteban could not have broken his word, not even if he'd known what waited at the end of the trail.

Then Chakoh was thrown to the ground. He pushed himself to hands and knees and rose unsteadily to his feet. Before him stretched his shadow, a shadow arrow in its side. Hot moisture ran down his thigh. His fingers traced it curiously to his side and felt the shaft. As yet there was no pain, just a numb acceptance that something unusual had happened to him.

Aunt Maria's husband grabbed his arm. "Run!"

"Look, I have an arrow in my side."

"There is no time. Run!"

Chakoh let himself be dragged away. Dimly he remembered to tuck the rattle in the thong of his loincloth.

Of the more than a hundred Pima who had accompanied Esteban, only a handful remained. They met Fray Marcos two days' journey down the trail and reported the tragedy at Cíbola.

There was little Chakoh could remember of the flight from Cíbola. Weariness, hunger, the pain from the wound in his side, and a blur of voices and hands. Fray Marcos' strong bony hands urging him forward; Aunt Maria's gentle ones tending him and her voice husky with worry and urging him to stay. Then his own voice, strange in his ears, insisting on returning to Mexico with Fray Marcos. He must have had his way, for in the red blur of pain he remembered the litter that carried him to Culiacán, the unbearable jostling of horses, then mercifully nothing until he roused to the dull thud of horse hoofs on the causeways. Then came the whispers, many whispers, and in the background the clicking of prayer beads. Then they too were lost in the hot waves of pain and fever.

THIRTEEN ❋ "GO WITH GOD"

The sun had taken the night chill from the Plaza. From his seat at the convent window Chakoh watched the robed priests, the Indians in short white mantles, and the over-dressed Spaniards that thronged the marketplace. Horses pushed slowly through the crowd. One shied at the banner carried by a court page. All Mexico had gathered for the fiesta and not one among them could Chakoh call friend.

Brother Solano bustled into the room. "I am sorry to be late, but there's a great to-do in the kitchen today."

He gathered the plates of untouched food from the table, scolding Chakoh gently. "You live by the grace of God, but the Lord cannot help you if you do not eat."

"I am not hungry."

"You cannot watch a fiesta on an empty stomach. I'll leave the apricots and yam cakes."

Chakoh smiled. During the day Brother Solano would send more baskets and platters from the kitchen, tempting his appetite with everything the garden or market provided. By sundown he would be surrounded by food for which had no taste. How strange was life. Hunger had brought him to Mexico. Now he had food and could not eat.

There were whispers outside the room. Fray Marcos walked briskly across the floor and felt Chakoh's head.

"The wound is healing; the fever has gone but you must eat, my son. You cannot live on an empty stomach."

"Or with an empty heart."

"I know how you feel. I lost many friends when I was with Pizarro in Peru, but the sadness passes."

"To be sure." The familiar words tightened his throat and the emptiness inside him grew. "He was alone and far from home. Who will mourn him?"

"I will pray for his soul." But the priest's tone showed he considered it a duty. It was not grief that prompted the prayers for a disobedient slave.

Dorantes would certainly grieve but only for a valuable

possession that he had lost. Only Cabeza de Vaca might bow his head a moment when he heard. Esteban was so far from his own land and his own people. There was no one to light the funeral pyre and chant the death song.

And if I had died from my wound, thought Chakoh, who would have lit mine?

He straightened in the chair and reached for a yam cake. Fray Marcos nodded approvingly and began to tell of the great army Coronado was to lead against Cíbola. Already men were flocking to sign under his banner. But Chakoh heard other words, another voice.

Can you bear arms in the service of the King? Or do you have a trade to serve those who do bear arms? What will you do in Mexico, little one?

As if in answer to his despair, he remembered: "My hut will be empty until you return."

Aunt Maria had said it, but it was not her hut that Chakoh saw. He rose abruptly and began piling his few possessions on the large bed: the medicine bag, Esteban's rattle, the bow that had gathered dust since he first came to Mexico.

"My son," exclaimed Fray Marcos, "what are you doing?"

"I am going home." He glared at the priest, defying him to stop his return. Fray Marcos pulled thoughtfully at his lower lip.

"Yes, that is best for you. But not now. You are too weak for such a long journey."

"I am strong enough to travel as far as Aunt Maria's. I shall rest there and learn the planting songs and the way of growing things. Then I shall trade for seeds to take with me to my people."

There would never be any question of what he could do among his own people. He would be a warrior, a hunter, and in time, the headman of his village. His heart would be full, and with the earth magic of the Pima his people could fill their stomachs.

Fray Marcos rose and placed his hands on Chakoh's shoulders. "Do not forget your prayers. Teach them to your people. Someday we shall come to you. Perhaps not in your time or even in your son's. But we shall come and build a church."

"You will be welcome."

"I shall ask Brother Solano to prepare food for your journey. He will also give you seeds from our garden." The priest drew his rosary from his belt. "Take this with you. Remember it was prayer that saved your life. Go with God, my son."

He made the sign of the cross and hurried from the room. Chakoh slipped the praying beads into the medicine bag with the last few tea leaves, the deer-hoof rattle, and the two blue stones he planned to trade to the Pima for seeds.

"The need is great," he whispered.

He had more difficulty with his farewells in the kitchen.

Brother Solano tried to persuade him to stay. His last argument was of the dangers.

"One boy alone with all those heathens. You will be killed, lad. It was hard enough with the four men when you came. How can you travel it alone?"

"I go with God," answered Chakoh. "And I *must* return."

Esteban had shown him that. He had wanted freedom more than anything the Spaniards could have given. He would be among the Buffalo People now if he had not kept his word and finished his mission.

Chakoh could do no less.

When Brother Solano saw his pleas had no effect, he tried to load Chakoh with more food than the boy could possibly carry. When at last he walked into the Plaza the last of the crowd was shuffling into the arena for the bullfights.

Esteban had often tried to describe the fights, but Chakoh could never imagine them as anything other than the Man-Chased-by-Buffalo. He stood in the empty Plaza remembering the first time he had seen Esteban do the pantomime.

Trumpets blared in the arena. The crowd cheered. Chakoh could almost see Esteban entering the Plaza, mincing and bowing with the buffalo robe over his shoulder.

More trumpets. More cheers.

Esteban cavorted now as the buffalo, now as the hunter.

Chakoh saw him clearly in the center of the Plaza swinging the robe, thrusting with the stone knife and then, as the buffalo, sprawling on the stones and kicking his legs. But this time the "buffalo" did not rise but sat up, dusted the paving, and lay down as if to sleep.

"Olé! Olé!" rose from the arena.

The vision faded with the cheers. There was nothing in the Plaza but the litter of the fiesta.

Chakoh dropped his bundles and bow, and ran back to the abbey kitchen. Brother Solano looked up in surprise but said nothing when Chakoh gathered fuel and an ember from the fire. He carried them to the center of the deserted Plaza, to the spot where Esteban as the buffalo had lain down to die.

The fire was small but large enough for the purpose. When it burned brightly Chakoh unfastened the gourd rattle from his waistband and laid it gently atop the flames. The feathers blazed and were gone. The gourd crackled and spit as it burned. Chakoh watched until there was nothing left of the precious rattle. Nothing left to bind Esteban's spirit to this foreign land. Then Chakoh raised both arms above his head, faced the land of the rising sun, and began to chant.

He sang of a spirit wandering far from its home. He begged forgiveness for having no more possessions to add to the fire but the Dark One had been poor in life. He had walked the world with nothing but a great heart, and that he had shared with many. The chant ended with a plea to release Esteban's spirit from this strange land. "Let it find rest in the land of his fathers."

Through the wispy smoke he thought he saw Esteban leaping and cavorting as the buffalo chased the hunter. He blinked and the vision was gone.

"Farewell, my friend. Go with God."

Then he shouldered his bow, picked up his bundles, and spat twice over his left shoulder. The medicine bag swung full and heavy against his thigh as he strode out over the causeway. He did not look back.

✳ BIBLIOGRAPHY

BARCA, FRANCES CALDERÓN DE LA, *Life in Mexico*. Garden City, New York, Doubleday & Co., 1960.

HALLENBECK, CLEVE, *Álvar Núñez Cabeza de Vaca*. Glendale, California, The Arthur H. Clark Co., 1940.

VACA, CABEZA DE, *Adventures in the Unknown Interior of America*, edited and translated by Cyclone Covey. New York, The Crowell-Collier Publishing Co., 1961.

✳ ABOUT THE AUTHOR

Betty Baker's first book for Harper & Row was LITTLE RUN-
NER OF THE LONGHOUSE, an I CAN READ BOOK about the Iroquois
Indians' New Year celebration. It was followed by THE
SHAMAN'S LAST RAID, a humorous story about present-day
Apache twins; KILLER-OF-DEATH, which deals with the more
serious problems of a young Apache brave in the 19th Cen-
tury and which won the Western Heritage Award for the
best book for children in 1963; and THE TREASURE OF THE
PADRES, a contemporary story of life in the Southwest.

Betty Baker was born in Bloomsburg, Pennsylvania, and has
lived in various cities in New Jersey. Now a confirmed West-
erner by adoption, she lives in Tucson, Arizona. An in-
veterate reader since the age of four, she first used what she
considered her inexhaustible supply of extraneous knowledge by writing acrostic puzzles. Later, her active participa-
tion in the interests of her young son led her to write her
first book for children. When Harper & Row asked her if
she wished to include a dedication in KILLER-OF-DEATH, she
replied, "This book needs no dedication. It *is* one." That this
statement is true of more than one of Betty Baker's books is
clear to all her readers.